Dancing in the Dark

'*Dancing in the Dark* is a compelling, deeply affecting
read. Prendergast has captured such an authentic
teenage girl's voice ... Certainly one of the best Irish teen
novels I've read this year and bang on the zeitgeist.'

Sarah Webb, author of the 'Amy Green' series

P.R. PRENDERGAST is a secondary school teacher in Dublin and has also written *The Romanian Builder*, for younger readers.

Dancing in the Dark

P.R. Prendergast

THE O'BRIEN PRESS
DUBLIN

First published 2010 by The O'Brien Press Ltd,
12 Terenure Road East, Rathgar, Dublin 6, Ireland.
Tel: +353 1 4923333; Fax: +353 1 4922777
E-mail: books@obrien.ie
Website: www.obrien.ie

ISBN: 978-1-84717-185-6

British Library Cataloguing-in-publication Data
A catalogue record for this title is available from the British Library

1 2 3 4 5 6 7 8 9 10
10 11 12 13 14 15

The O'Brien Press receives
assistance from

Cover image: iStockphoto
Printed by CPI Cox and Wyman Ltd.
The paper in this book is produced using pulp from managed forests.

As ever, for Trish, Conor, Joe and Orla

Author's Note

*D*ancing in the Dark began its life as a musical, to be performed by the Fifth Form at the school where I teach. I had hoped to write a story that offered exciting roles for both boys and girls, for kids who could sing and for those who couldn't, and which might accurately reflect teenage life. The play was an overwhelming success, but after the final curtain came down I was left thinking about the characters and wondering if I had made the most of that story. Without the constraint of writing a musical, something at which I had no prior experience, could I have told the story in a richer and more challenging way? This novel is an attempt to do that. I hope you enjoy it.

P.R. Prendergast

Nine-thirty, getting towards the end of my homework and James appears. And when I say appears, I mean *appears*.

'Hey up, little sis,' he says.

Cat got my tongue? he wants to know. Or maybe I'm just pretending not to hear him.

'Listen,' I say, 'how come I see more of you now than I did when you were alive?'

I ask him is there anyone else and he says anyone else who? Anyone else that you appear to, you moron? That you pester. Maybe that was my mistake, after all – I answered him. The trick would have been to stay shtum, wait for him to hoof off again.

'That how it works?' I ask. 'You just say something to someone and they hear you? What about the old pair?'

'What about them?'

'Why not treat them to your sparkling wit?'

'It would upset them too much,' he says. 'They have to get used to living without me.'

'And I don't?'

'You find this upsetting?' he wants to know.

'I find it irritating.'

'Well, if that's the case I'll take myself off,' he says and before I can say, *Don't let me keep you*, he's gone, puff, just vanished into thin air.

I sit and stare at the space he's just vacated and wonder if that's the last I've seen of him. Wouldn't that be something!

Only of course it's not.

Two minutes later and he's back again.

'Hey up,' he says again.

'Long time no see.'

He makes as if to flick through my book, only his hand passes through it.

'What's this? History? Don't worry about history,'

he says. 'It all happened years ago.' He points to a sheet of paper on my desk. 'What's this?'

'We've to write a poem.'

'A poem?'

'English class. A limerick. Five lines, minimum number of rhymes – two. Want to hear?'

'Sure,' he says and then he does this big cough like he's clearing his throat and he introduces me. 'Poem, by Jessie Dunn,' he says.

'Okay then.' I pretend to read, but I'm really making it up. And I start. 'There's nothing quite as useless as a brother,' I tell him.

'That the first line?'

'You like it?'

'Not bad.'

'If anyone's to blame, it's his mother.'

'Good one,' he says.

'Look underneath your seat—'

'Go on.'

'You find his smelly size twelve feet—'

'I like it.'

'And now I'm rid of him I sure don't want another.'

He just looks at me with that big dopey grin of his. He looks ridiculous, still in the rugby gear he died in, only with his black school shoes underneath.

'Do you not have anywhere else to be?' I ask. 'I've to do my dance practice.'

He tells me that I'm already practising.

'Sorry?'

'Sitting. All they ever let you do is sit on the bench so you're doing fine as you are.'

'Well, maybe if I practise some more they might let me dance,' I tell him.

'It must be such a disappointment to Mum and Dad,' he says and he looks away into the distance like he's remembering something from years ago. 'Your brother having been such a star and all. He feints, he sees the gap, he goes. Remember how good I was? I lit up that school, let me tell you. One sway of these hips and the guy who was marking me would buy the dummy and so did the other players, they bought it and even my own team mates and the crowd, they'd all shift slightly—'

'Is there not someone over there on your side of things who'd be happy to listen to this stuff?' I ask him.

He shrugs. 'I wish there was.'

'Because I had a bellyful of it when you were alive and I don't see why I should have to listen to it now. I'll tell you what, I'll just close my eyes and count to ten and then when I open them you'll be gone. How about that?'

'You really want me to go?'

'See? I knew you'd get it. That bang on the head really sharpened you up.'

'No pretence then.'

'That's right. No pretence. We never got along when you were alive, did we? So why should we get along now? We both know where we stand.'

'You said it, Jess. We both know.'

I close my eyes and wait. Is he gone yet? Time's ticking and there's some dance moves I need to practise for tomorrow. Mum and Dad are downstairs watching telly, Mum on the couch, Dad in the armchair, both, as you might imagine, overwhelmed with grief by the loss of their eldest child, their only son. Six months next Tuesday. Back when it happened every minute was like slow drip torture and you think they'll never pass, but they do, the minutes passing into hours, the days into weeks, all the while you think it might get easier. Only it never does. Then finally into months. Six of them. Hard to believe that we could have spent six months without James, but we have. His helmet was hanging from the handlebars of his bike, that was the stupidest thing.

There was a strong family resemblance between James and Dad, the same chunkiness of build, the same lego-shaped head perfect for slotting into a scrum. Dad's a former rugby international himself.

And Mum? Well, there are no words for what Mum's going through at the moment. Want to know what she does? She exists. She breathes in and she breathes out. One day and then the next. Pack lunch for school, dinner at six, I always have clean clothes. She functions. But pick any moment of the day and she's thinking of James or she's just been thinking of James or she's just about to think of James. I hear her ask about other people, how they're getting on, how their kids are. And she's interested. She's that sort of person. She wants to know. But most of her died that evening with James. 'Shellmum', that's what I call her. Tip her and she might crack. Shellmum and Shelldad, the shellparents.

Most of the time I just don't know what to say to them.

When I open my eyes James has finally shoved off with himself.

Less than a fortnight until the national finals. Most of the time I think, *Thank God I'm only a sub*. The pressure would be too much for me. I flick on the music and begin to dance.

2

Cereal for brekkie. I could of course tell them, I suppose. Dad with his noggin stuck in the paper, but Mum would listen. It was always me and Mum. Stands to reason with a couple of rugby meatheads in the family, the pair of them heading off to matches or training or else stuck in front of the box discussing the timing of the pass or some such waffle.

Hey, Mum? I could say.

Yes, love?

Only what then? *James came back last night? He comes every night,* I could tell them. *He's in my room right now if you want to nip up and say hello.*

And they'd have me carted off to the nuthouse.

Breakfast used to be pretty lively around here,

James full of guff like he always was, stuffing toast down his gob and looking for his rugby gear. Dad trying to read the paper from the day before. Mum and I always had things to talk about. School, for instance, or the characters she worked with, or *ER* or *Grey's Anatomy* or some film we'd watched together.

We still talk, of course. But it's different now. Her voice is different; there's a real deadness to it. Soon I won't be able to remember how she used to sound. That's one of the worst things, I'm afraid. Sometimes I wonder if she will ever manage to give herself fully to anything again.

Off to school. Nothing like a little education, after all. Three and a half grand a year to send your kid to a nice private school like this one, which in my case might be money well spent, but I don't think anything ever penetrated that thick skull of James's. Still, there was always the ruggah, wasn't there?

One good thing about this place; it's within walking

distance. And I can collect my friend Rhona on the way. There used to be more of us. There used to be Louisa and Amanda and Lizzie and Rhona and me and Jessica and Katelyn, and a couple of others who'd come and go. But this was the main gang. There's all sorts of groups within a school year. You have your nerds and your jocks. You have your goths and your rockers. You have your emos and your skateboarders. It's important to have your group. Find yourself without a group and people begin to wonder why. Once they begin to wonder why they don't want you in their group.

Yeah, like I say there used to be quite a gang of us. Now it's just me and Rhona together.

First thing she says is, 'Geography.'

I flip my copy out of the bag.

'Word for word?' she asks.

'Word for word. There's no way he's going to read it. You try the maths?'

'Why would I try it if I'm not able to do it?'

You have to admire the logic.

'She's likely to check that more closely. I'll show you where to go wrong.'

And we continue on our way. Rhona is a talker and she's just getting into her stride, how her parents are expecting her to put some order on that room of hers and not a word about payment, if I can believe that, when we hear someone call out,

'Hi, girls!'

Not just 'Hi, girls.' More like 'Hi, girls, I'm the new kid and am I not just the coolest thing you've ever seen?' Only you can see he's a dork straight away. Our age, but tall for it with his hair gelled up and the knot of his school tie halfway down his chest the way we all do. His blazer's crumpled like he spent ten minutes jumping up and down on it once he got out of his mother's sight.

'I'm Alan,' he says and then he gives us this look. 'But you can call me Al. You girls in Third Year?'

'Don't worry what year we're in,' Rhona says.

'What year are you in?'

'Third.'

'Then you can't go into school like that. You got a hair brush?' she asks me.

'Use your own hair brush,' I tell her.

'All right, you do the tie.'

Alan, *Al*, wants to know what's wrong with his tie and Rhona explains that it's too low and the last thing he needs on his first day is a uniform infringement. Especially since the first thing any new kid does is report to his form teacher.

'Don't worry about our ties', I explain, 'we're veterans of the system. We're lost causes.'

And anyway, a form teacher comes across a new kid looking like he's been here a year and he's going to assume he's trouble. To satisfy Rhona I grab his tie and give it a good yank, half choking the poor fella. And Rhona in no time has brushed his hair right over; she's given him a terrific side part. In less than ten seconds we've transformed him from teenage rebel wannabe to an eight-year-old making his First Communion.

'That's much better, Alan,' Rhona says. 'Now you're ready for the school day.'

'You girls want to walk in together?'

'Not today we don't,' I tell him. 'This girl here has yet to start her homework.'

Each day it's the same. I wonder if James has finally hoofed off into the other world and then he appears.

Usually it's when I'm on my way to the school gym.

Each morning I use the gym. It's empty. It's quiet. I can put on my music and dance.

Only today there's no sign of the big lunkhead. Where is he? Maybe he's gone for good. Wouldn't that be something? Usually he's here at this hour rattling on about how there should be a life-size sculpture of him in the main foyer. And another here maybe. Fitting reminders of his greatness, as he puts it. There's no shortage of photos, mind you; as you walk into the gym there's a whole series of them. James making a break. James dumping some poor chap on his back. James lifting the the Leinster Junior Cup. He thinks maybe it's the shame of only being a sub on the dance team that drives me on. Must be tough, he always says, following in the steps of a star, the finest sportsman the school has known.

Only today I'm spared the school's finest sportsman. What I get instead is the finest dancer in the history of our school.

'Don't worry,' Louisa Bennett says, 'we can wait.' I didn't hear them come in. Louisa Bennett, school captain, national champion, national captain, here today with my old chums Amanda and Lizzie. This time last year we were inseparable, but things change, don't they? They're welcome to the space, but, no, they won't hear of it. Happy to watch, they say. I was here first, after all; and we're all part of the same team, remember. Their voices are like syrup, their expressions like glass.

I want to leave. But I don't want to run from them. I have no choice but to continue.

Only it's hard to dance with them watching. This retro *Grease* piece Miss Smyth has us practising for the nationals is a tricky one, much trickier than it seemed last night in my room when the spins and steps seemed manageable and I know it's not right, my timing is wrong, the steps are wrong. If I keep going I'm likely to end up on my ear so I do the only sensible thing and stop.

'Lovely to see,' Louisa says. 'Such dedication to the craft. You know what my international coach says?'

'What?'

'He says a team's only as good as its weakest link.'

I sigh. 'And that's me?'

'No,' Louisa says. 'You're not even *on* the team. You're sub.'

Amanda makes this wincing noise, like that one really stung and she's feeling my pain. The same

Amanda who not so long ago was my closest friend.

'The problem,' Louisa explains, 'is that there might be an injury and then the team would only be as good as its weakest link and, to be honest, that's not very good, is it?'

I have some thinking to do, they reckon.

It's not that they don't want me or anything, they're happy to assure me, it's just that they worry.

National finals on the way and all, do I really want to be the one who mucks the whole thing up?

Not just for them.

For the whole school.

All the work that has gone into it. When will they have the chance again?

It's not that I can't dance, Louisa explains. I can dance … a bit. It's just, you know, like how her international coach always says, there's some people who always, like, let you down. They just don't have the right character to perform. Nothing against them or anything, it's just the way they are.

She gives me the sweetest smile.

'Why don't you scoot along with yourself now?' she says.

'Tarrah now,' says Amanda.

'Cheerio,' says Lizzie.

'Think about what we said,' says Louisa.

3

S till no sign.

Where is the useless lump? Big dope, just like when he was alive, always around when you don't need him and then when you might like to say, *Hey, what do you think their problem is?* you think there'd be any sign of him?

Not a chance.

Still, there's always plenty to look at on a school corridor. No gratitude, that's what's wrong with kids these days. Offer ten seconds of your morning to make sure a new kid is nerded up nicely and what does he do only try to make himself look cool again! Only nobody is fooled. Not the students and not the teachers and certainly not the hoolies, 'hoolie' being short for 'hooligan', Richie Robinson at the helm.

Richie the pusher. Richie the intimidator. Richie with more than a threat of violence to back it up. Fat kids, skinny kids, kids with something to hide, Richie will fit you in if he can find the time.

And now he's found the time for Alan.

Just a brush of the shoulders to begin with. Richie's old school.

'You touch me?' he says. He turns to the rest of the morons. 'He touch me?'

Alan tries to bluff it out.

'Hey, guys,' he says. 'I'm Al.'

As if they give a damn who he is. Richie pokes Alan in the chest. Max Birchall shoves him back again.

'You talking to me now?' Richie wants to know. 'Who do you think you are, talking to me? I say you could talk to me? And you sure as hell don't touch me. I can touch you though. You got a problem with that?'

Richie jabs him in the chest again.

'I didn't hear you.'

'Yes,' Alan says.

'Yes what?'

'Yes, I don't have a problem with that.'

They all laugh. 'You mean, no, you don't have a problem with that. English your first language? You see me? Well, next time you see me you cross the corridor. You got that?'

I can see Alan puff his chest out; he's trying to gather his courage, but it won't come. Maybe there's just not any of it there, and his shoulders bunch over. Richie up to his old tricks again. Richie likes new kids. He has a talent for sizing them up. Maybe he can recruit them. Maybe he can torment them. Either way they're worth checking out.

We all hoped that once he started going out with Louisa he might leave everyone else alone. Only it hasn't really worked out like that.

'You got that?' he says to Alan.

'I got it.'

'I didn't hear you.'

'I got it.'

Quick as a flash Richie flicks a finger into Alan's eye. Not a poke, a lightning quick flick and Alan reels backwards.

'Well, that's good,' Richie says and he leads his cronies away.

Alan just stands, stunned. *Same as his last school?* I can't help but wonder. Some kids just can't help themselves. The fear radiates from them, the desperation to belong. And every school's got a Richie, I reckon.

In ways it's easier for the goths. Or the rockers, or the emos, or the nerds. Those groups are clearly defined. You're in because of who you are, what you like, how you choose to look. And more importantly, no one else wants to be in.

It is amongst the rest of us that the problems arise. Alliances form, break up, reform differently. Boys are different, maybe. They seem to thump each other and get on with things. With girls, though, it's trickier to read. You're never quite sure whether or not the ground is shifting under your feet.

I've seen it happen before. A girl is in until she's out; once she's out there's no way back in. I watch her wander bewildered and confused. What has happened? Why is today different from yesterday? She has to be patient; there are other groups after all, other girls, other friendships to be made. She just has to lick her wounds and get on with things.

It's the shock that kills you.

Sometimes I think I should never have joined the dance team. Yeah, maybe that was the mistake; everything was fine up to that point. Me and Rhona and Amanda, the three of us next to inseparable, Amanda hitting it off with Louisa and Lizzie and a couple of others. Amanda and Louisa are in the same dance class. Louisa and Lizzie are best friends from primary school.

And Rhona? First day in Junior Infants and there

was Rhona, her hair done in braids. She was wearing a yellow dress with puffy sleeves. My knees were knocking under the table. She pushed the Snakes & Ladders across the table and said, 'Red's my favourite, but you could be red if you like.'

I took blue. Best pals, right from day one.

This time last year I gave us all a name – 'The Normals'.

It was kind of thrilling sitting there in the canteen listening to Lizzie and Louisa tearing strips off some of the others. The rockers and the emos and the goths, who did they think they were kidding? At least with the nerds there was no pretending. Mind you, Louisa said, had we noticed there were some serious weight issues amongst the nerds?

Had anyone seen the spot on the end of Claire Fitzgerald's chin? Something like that appears and the thing to do is bury yourself in the bed for a week.

And Aoife O'Neill's stammer? Anyone else feel

like giving her a slap and saying, *Spit it out, girl?*

I had never heard anyone talk about other people like this. It made me uncomfortable. At the same time it thrilled me though I hate to admit that now. If they're out, you're in. You're well and truly in.

The question was: what to call ourselves?

It was out of my mouth before I could stop it: 'The Normals'.

Implying what? That the others were abnormal. What a thing to say! Kids could like whatever clothes or hairstyles or music or books they wanted as far as I was concerned. What did I care? But I'd said it and it was out there.

The others loved it.

Yeah, The Normals, that was it. High fives all round and way to go, Jess, good one, and hey, wasn't it about time I tried out for the dance team? Especially since, according to Amanda, all I ever did was dance. What did I mean I just danced for the sake of it? What was the point in that? It'd be the thing to do, join the team since, well, there were some right donkeys in there. It'd be fun. There would be more of the gang on the team. Thirteen girls, eight boys, if nothing else I'd make it an even number. Jazz, hip-hop, tap and even a bit of salsa – Miss Smyth's routines could be corny, but there was something for everyone.

It was Amanda who kept on about it. It was she who said, 'See, I told you so,' when I made the grade.

It was she who said, 'Gee, I didn't expect you to be that good.'

It was she who really turned on me.

One thing about James, he was friendly. A big useless dope, let there be no doubt about that, but he certainly was friendly. New kid in the school and he'd walk straight over and say, *Hi, I'm James Dunn, you've probably read about me in the papers.* People loved him for it. Some kid on his own and he'd fire the ball in his direction. *Hey you, play on the other team, see can we make a game of this.* When I came to this school and folks heard I was James Dunn's sister they all expected me to be some sort of super athlete as well. They seemed disappointed to find that I was just ordinary. And relieved in a way. Like Louisa says, it's not that I can't dance. I can dance … a bit. That's what I'm thinking of when Alan appears again at my shoulder saying, 'Hey, it's Geography now, I think.'

'I'd love to sit next to you,' I tell him, 'but there's a little informal arrangement here. Eggheads, that's me, over one side. Thickos, jocks and other assorted wasters over the other. Until you prove otherwise that's where you're headed.'

I lead him over and plonk him into a desk that's usually empty. And when I get back to my own place who's there only James with that usual dopey grin, still in the same rugby gear with the black leather shoes.

'You're late,' I say.

'Teacher's not here yet,' Rhona says.

'I wasn't talking to you.'

She sighs. 'Not this again,' she says.

Which means I have to be quiet. It embarrasses Rhona when other kids come up and say, 'Your friend's going crazy, she's always talking to herself.' Not that Rhona minds too much otherwise.

'Maybe it's normal,' she says, 'imagining your brother has come back to see you.'

How is she meant to know? She's never had anyone die on her. And she's not a shrink. She just wishes I'd shut up when we're out in public. So now I'll have to listen to James without being able to tell him to shut his piehole. Which is not easy, let me say. It's hard to believe that so much rubbish can come out of one mouth. He comes and goes through the day; some classes he likes more than others. History he enjoys, for whatever reason since he never did when he was alive. Sometimes he curls up on one of the shelves and goes asleep. Other times he occupies an empty desk. He seldom lasts the forty minutes. A couple of days ago what did he do in the middle of

Science class only shout, 'How can anyone be expected to listen to this garbage?' and launch himself out the lab window. Even I have to admit that it was pretty funny. Three times in a row he did it before the teacher suggested I step outside, see could I compose myself.

Just because he's an idiot doesn't mean he can't be funny every now and then.

You'd want to have seen his funeral, though. Packed to the gills that church was; even the grounds were full and down the street there were lines of people. Some lads from the rugby team carried his coffin inside; others formed a guard of honour outside. Every now and then the service would be punctuated with a great racking sob from somewhere amongst the congregation. And then the graveyard. God, the graveyard! Desolate, that's the only word, the rain bouncing like a hail of arrows on the lid of his coffin. No one sobbed. No one cried out. Have I ever felt so cold? We just watched in aching disbelief as a prayer was uttered and the coffin slid from view.

I thought I would never see him again.

It took six weeks.

For six weeks I walked in the worst kind of fog. There was a deadness inside me, in my bones, in my blood. I breathed in, I breathed out. I listened to the dry ticking of the seconds as they passed. Agonising, no other word for it, the days turning to weeks. Then it was three in the morning and I was lying awake staring that same empty stare at the same set of curtains and all of a sudden there he was.

'Hey sis,' he said. 'Missing me yet?' He looked over at my desk. 'I see you haven't changed your nerdy ways,' he said. All that stuff going on with the girls, why didn't I tell him about it when he was around to help? 'Go back to sleep,' he said, 'I haven't gone far.'

I was sure I was dreaming.

Only it wasn't a dream. The next night he was back again. And the next one. He comes and goes as he pleases.

And now here in school today he's looking at me again.

Bruges, the teacher tells us, is known as the Venice of the north because of its many canals and James looks over with this big inane grin on his face as if to say, *Well now, isn't that an interesting and enlightening point?*

He throws a glance in the direction of the window as though he might throw himself out again. Only he doesn't. He just shrugs and settles himself into the seat. He has the look of a guy who has nowhere else to be and is going to rest up a while.

I look back to the board and take down a few notes.

4

There's quite a kerfuffle in the changing room, all the girls agog at Louisa's new ring. A genuine ruby, apparently, and God knows what it cost. Richie wouldn't tell her. All he said was that she deserved it, beautiful girl like her; she could think of it as a good luck charm what with the dance finals coming up in a week or two. And to be fair, it is a beautiful ring. I can't help thinking that I wouldn't mind owning it. Only it would look much better on Louisa who, when she's not being obnoxious, is flat out the prettiest girl in the school.

Yes, pretty. You're in until you're out and that was one of the reasons they gave, by the way – I wasn't pretty enough. Something to do with my eyes apparently. In fact, now that they looked at them, could they even be sure they were a white person's eyes? They certainly had a foreign look about them. Which gives you an idea of how low Louisa and her chums are willing to stoop. Yeah, my eyes and my hips; there was something funny about the way I walked as well. Catch me at the right angle and you'd be doing well not to burst out laughing.

Louisa, on the other hand, never looks prettier than when she's dancing.

Such elegance! I always think. Such poise! Sometimes she takes our breath away. Mostly it's her timing that sets her apart, all that fluidity perfectly controlled. Her parents spotted her talent when she was still a tot and nurtured it, hired private coaches, fired those coaches and hired others, and what we have here is a champion, someone who is on the way to greatness. Louisa is to be cherished. That's what Miss Smyth says. We should appreciate Louisa, cherish her. She will lead the school to glory. We should watch her closely, learn from her.

Now, however, the girls are learning how to model a ring, show it in all its splendour. Richie had a big day at the racetrack, apparently. It is illegal for under eighteens to bet, but apparently that's not such a problem if you can get better odds behind the scenes and that's what she's explaining to everyone when Miss Smyth barrels on in and tells us time's a-ticking, there's a national final coming up.

I sit alone, lace up my dance shoes. Always alone, it's like I have my own corner. Not that I blame the others. We all know how it works. Some people are in and some are out and the last thing you want is to align yourself too closely with someone who's out. It's not that they're hostile. Best way to describe it is that they're just not friendly. They answer my question but that's it, they never ask me one in return. It took me a while to figure it out. I make them nervous. I make them uneasy. They wish it was different, I'm sure, but it's not, so if it's all the same to me they'd rather I just kept to myself.

And out we troop.

Starters to the floor, subs to the bench. That's how it works.

Sub, sub, sub – a girl could get sick of this and maybe it shows on my face because Miss Smyth says, 'No, no, that's not right, Jessie. You have to look eager. Look interested. Team effort, remember! Impression is everything and the judges will be examining every aspect of the performance. There's no "I" in "team", is there?' she asks.

'No, but there's two in "idiot",' I mutter under my breath.

'Sorry?'

'I said I'll get the hang of it.'

She looks at me dubiously, but lets it go because all of a sudden Clodagh Ryan has her hand up.

'I have to go, Miss,' Clodagh says.

My heart jumps. Miss Smyth looks exasperated. 'What is it *this* time? You were at the dentist last week.'

'The doctor.'

'The doctor?'

'I have a rash. Just here,' she says and moves the top of her tracksuit from her hip and Miss Smyth wheels away in horror and says, 'No thank you, that's quite as much as I need to know. Jessie,' she says, 'step in.'

And I spring from the bench. It's either me or Nikki Finch and Nikki's likely to fall off the stage if you leave her up there long enough.

Reprieve! Stupid isn't it? You wait all week for something, practise hour after hour in your bedroom or alone in the gym, and then when the opportunity comes it fills you with dread. Your heart jumps, your stomach churns. But you don't have time to think about any of that because you step into action.

Grease. Dad bought me the DVD so I could watch how it was first done. In my bedroom I can do it either way, the first one with Olivia Newton John or this new arrangement Miss Smyth has come up with, which allows room for Louisa to do her stuff. And she does it brilliantly, even I have to admit it. Every step, every movement. The rest of us offer back up and then she and Daniel Block play off each other and then she's moving in and out between us. And I'm really getting into it. When I dance everything else seems to fade, the steps and the beat, everything in synch; it's like you're part of something much stronger than yourself, some force maybe. Everything in sequence, each perfect movement making the next one easier until it's as though you're watching it all unfold before you, the dance as it was choreographed, as you bring it to life.

Only then I go and clip Louisa.

Stupid, stupid, stupid!

Or else she clips me.

I'm sure I have the step right, the timing perfect but still there is the slightest contact, and we're both fairly moving at this point so we both go flying.

I turn, bewildered.

'Stop the music,' Miss Smyth shouts.

Louisa is first to her feet.

'How am I meant to work under these conditions?' she screams and storms away towards the benches. Miss Smyth nearly tramples me in the rush to console her.

Yes, it can happen very suddenly all right.

Like I said, you're in until you're out. And you never see the signs.

If you're lucky they let you go quietly.

In my case it was in full view, in the school canteen, the gang of us sitting there during the early morning break just shooting the breeze like usual. Lizzie had a sore toe so she was wearing these bright white runners. They looked funny under her school uniform.

'You didn't mug a nurse on the way here by any chance?' I said.

And that was the spark. An innocent little comment, nothing more, just one in a line of comments and Amanda launched into it. Just like that. Without warning. She had a couple of things to say to me, she said, things that had been on everyone's mind for some time now.

Did I really think I was funny?

That was the biggest one: Did I really think I was funny?

Had I any idea how mind-numbingly boring it was listening to me, listening to the same rubbish day after day? She couldn't even begin to describe how sick of me they all were.

Everyone was staring at us. The canteen, it was quiet as a graveyard.

And she continued on. Some sort of insect, that's what I was, sucking every bit of blood out of the gang. Sometimes it was hard to even breathe with me constantly on their heels. A stray dog, that's what I was like, some sort of stray dog. Had I no sense? Was I blind or stupid, that was the question, or was it a combination of both?

Me just standing there – my face on fire with the shame of it, that horrible burning feeling at the back of my eyes from holding back the tears.

Finished, she said. Any friendship I'd ever imagined between us all, it was finished now. Or was I too thick to understand that?

You don't want to, but you can't help yourself. You know you have this desperate, pleading expression on your face when you look to the others for support. Rhona – absent this particular day. The others just waved me away. Louisa, smug, turning her head. Amanda screaming, 'Can you not just stay the hell away from us??'

The rest of lunch-break I spent in the bathroom. I splashed water on my eyes before I went back to class so they wouldn't seem so red.

It takes a few days for the stories to emerge.

Had anyone seen me at the weekend? Someone should tell those parents of mine there are clothes shops in the city other than Penneys and Dunnes.

My phone? Well, the best that could be said about it was that it matched my jewellery – they were both cheap crap.

There was the thing with my hips, wasn't there? That's why I was always half a step off when I danced.

Best of all was how James and I weren't real brother and sister. See how unalike we were! He didn't have those slanty, foreign eyes. Word had it that, and this wasn't to be repeated mind, but my Mum had gone on some foreign holiday and hooked up with some guy over there. Some guy she met straight off the plane.

Yes, the stories emerge, but they take a while to gain momentum. For the moment all that's facing me is the long walk.

I'm out.

I'm history.

There's an adjustment to be made because all of a sudden I'm on my own.

5

Shellmum and Shelldad, the shellparents, having their dinner.

Munch, munch.

'How was school?'

'School was fine, Dad.'

'How was dance practice?'

'Dance was fine, Mum.'

And then it's up to my room, to where the old Spudhead is waiting for me.

'What was for dins?' he says.

'Chops,' I say.

'Chops,' he says, 'not really one of my favourites.'

I sit and do my homework.

He'd read a magazine only he can't hold the pages. I'd drag up the portable telly only it might encourage him to stay. He sits up on the windowsill a lot, watches the road below. Keeps me posted on the neighbours, as if I give a toss.

'What's it like?' I say after a while.

It takes him a moment to answer as though he knows what's coming and he's taking a moment to collect his thoughts.

'What's what like?'

'You know. Heaven and hell. The afterlife. Any pearly white gates? How about some old guy with a white beard? What's it like?'

'What's what like?'

'You know. Being dead.'

He thinks for a moment.

'I don't know,' he says. He goes quiet. 'It's lonely,' he says.

'What about the other dead people?'

'They're a bit cliquey, to be honest. Maybe you have to work your way in. At least I still have this world to watch, I suppose.'

'Why me?' I ask. 'Why come back to me? Can you appear to anyone you want?'

'I presume so. You're the only one I tried it with. I really miss Mum and Dad.'

'Me too,' I say.

'I miss school.'

'School? You were hopeless at school.'

He looks out the window again as he is talking. He misses his pals. He misses the company, all the people, the noise. He misses the teachers, even the ones who thought he was a pain in the neck. He really misses the rugby.

'The glory?'

'Maybe.'

'The adoring girls?'

'A little.'

'All those big gorillas lying on top of you in the mud? Getting your backside flicked every time you step out of the shower?'

'It's the respect I miss,' he says. 'I'm smarter now

than before I died. Did you notice?'

'Well you were starting from a pretty low baseline. Maybe you're just better able to judge things by what you miss the most.'

He clicks his fingers only they make no sound and points to me.

'That's right. You know all those things you associate with being really good at sport? The glory. The girls. Being presented with cups at assembly. I don't really miss that. But there's something else.'

'What?'

'When you walk in the dressing room. There's a big game on and you walk in and all of your team-mates are there and they look at you and think, *God I'm glad it's my dressing room he's walking into. He's on our team.* Who's the best dancer in the school, for instance?'

I don't even have to think about that one.

'Louisa Bennett.'

'The best singer?'

'Louisa.'

'Actor?'

'That would be Louisa.'

'And what do you think when she walks in the hall?'

'I think, *Oh God, not this stupid cow again.*'

James grins. Then he sighs and says, 'Well maybe that's not such a good example. But no one knows your worth like your teammates. They know. They know when they're struggling, you don't shout and moan and hide, you don't start whinging to the ref or making excuses, you take the ball and you break with it. You want to know the best feeling in the world?'

'What?'

'This is the ultimate, now. It's scoring in a big game. Not just a big game, a close big game. It's twelve-all. Your team-mates are knackered, they're dead on their feet, they're hanging on and they can't for the life of them think how they're going to score. And then you make a break. You see a gap because you understand the game better than anyone else, even though you're not smart in other ways, and there might only be a tiny bit of space, but you're strong and powerful and you've also got that balance and those dancing feet and all of a sudden you're into that gap and you know no one's going to catch you, it's sayonara baby, you're gone and there's no feeling in the world like it, it's like you're soaring and it doesn't matter how much everyone is screaming, it seems quiet in your head and you put the ball down and you turn and there are your mates looking at you and let me tell you there's no look in the world like it.'

He goes quiet for a moment. Everything seems so still. I imagine that I can hear him breathe.

'I shouldn't have died, Jess,' he says.

'No one young should die,' I say and he points over my shoulder and who's there only the shellmum herself. She's carrying a tray – milk and a sandwich and a chunk of chocolate cake. Nine o'clock – bang on time, same as every other night, Mum or Dad, one or the other. They've stopped asking who I've been talking to. I always just say that I was reciting a poem.

They worry about me. I don't seem to want to do much of anything, they've noticed. And it's true. Off to school, back home again; it's been six months since I've gone out anywhere. Before James died I used to head out each weekend. There might be a gang going to the cinema or the local shopping centre or if I was really up for a laugh I might turn up at the dance at the local rugby club. Now all I seem to do is to stay up here and dance. 'Taps', that's what Dad calls me sometimes. All he ever hears is that tap, tap, tap overhead.

They wonder would it improve things if I got a proper place on the dance team, but I tell them I'd just keep messing up. And anyway being on the team isn't that important. I just like dancing, after all – here or in the gym or on stage, it doesn't make much difference.

Sometimes when Dad comes up he gives me the Larry Duggan story, Larry being the equivalent of James thirty years ago only what did Larry do only bust his knee twenty minutes into the season and Dad took his place and never looked back. The message, of course, being: Don't lose faith.

Two days ago when Mum came up she asked if maybe it might help if I talked to someone – a psychologist maybe.

Dad says it's like a big hole has been ripped right through the centre of his heart and he knows it's never going to heal. Mum just shakes her head. For her there are no words.

I don't want to talk to any psychologist.

Tonight, when she is gone, James hops off his spot on the windowsill.

'Chocolate cake?' he says. 'Good to see standards haven't been dropping in my absence.'

'Yeah,' I tell him, 'and these days it usually lasts more than a couple of hours.'

Only he's not really listening. 'Hey, Jess,' he says, 'what is it exactly those girls you dance with have against you?'

And that's a hell of a question. Because once you're out, you're out.

And there's no way back in.

But first things first. As soon as they got rid of me they came to a decision. The Normals were no longer The Normals. Now they liked to think of themselves as 'The Specials'. I was relieved. It was a stupid name in the first place, a stupid thing to say.

The problem was, however: where do you go? Because that's what friends are, I suppose: they're like a blanket. They protect you from feeling lost. They protect you from being alone. You don't have to worry about where to be.

In class for instance, who do you sit next to?

If you're split into groups who do you go with?

The canteen is worst of all; once you have your food, what do you do then? Just wander from table to table asking, 'Is that place taken?'

Or find an empty table and sit on your own.

Which is what I did. I just sat and ate and watched the other tables fill up. Was it my imagination or was everyone staring? All the gang trooped in and settled into their usual spot, Louisa and Amanda and Lizzie and the others all as animated as ever, watching for Rhona, keeping her seat for her. Then Rhona, daft as ever, turning up halfway through the school day. They waved and called her over. Their smiles turned to something else when she walked straight past them.

I nearly burst into tears I felt so grateful. It made sense really.

Rhona who saw the funny side of everything.

Rhona who sometimes seemed ill at ease if unpleasant things were being said about others.

Rhona sat opposite me and said: 'All right, pal? Looks like it's just you and me for the time being.'

'Let's go,' James says. It's hard to get any train of

thought going with this clown knocking around.

'Go where?'

'Let's start. Let's get some practice in. I can help you. You want to get on that dance team, don't you?'

That's James for you: staring wistfully out the window one minute; all rugger bugger enthusiasm the next.

'Maybe I don't,' I tell him. 'Maybe that's why I keep screwing up.'

'So you won't have to dance?'

'So I won't have to dance with anyone watching me.'

He thinks for a moment. What he reckons is that those stupid cows on the dance team keep putting me off. Eat the pressure, that's his advice. It's all a matter of focus.

'Really?' I say.

'Absolutely.'

'Focus?'

'That's right. And now's the time to start.'

'Can I close my eyes?' I ask him.

'If you want.'

'Can I hum softly?'

He looks at me suspiciously. 'Are you going to take this seriously or not?'

'I'm having a bit of trouble,' I tell him. 'You're a ghost, remember?'

'So?'

'In rugby gear?'

'Well, I didn't have time to change. Here's my suggestion. You do remember my greatness, don't you?'

I let a loud sigh. 'How could I forget?'

'That combination of style and power and extraordinary natural talent.'

'I couldn't have put it better myself.'

'Well, here's something you probably didn't know. There was a large mental element to my greatness. The secret is to calm yourself. You have to build a wall around yourself.'

Sometimes it's hard not to laugh at the big lunkhead.

'Go on.'

'Close your eyes.'

'They're closed.'

'Relax your muscles.'

'They're relaxed.'

'Repeat after me: I am in control of the situation.'

I hold my hands out in front of me.

'Hang on,' I say. 'I'm getting a message from the other side. It must be your presence. The voice says: Your brother has ... a ... pile of wet cement between his ears.'

And I burst out laughing. James doesn't think it's so funny, mind you. He gives me this exasperated look and jumps up. He's wasting his time here, apparently. Some people just don't want to be helped. And then he vanishes. Just disappears through the wall.

'If only it was always that easy,' I call after him.

I laugh some more.

I wait. He's gone, it would seem. Often before he

goes each night he likes to mention some detail or incident from when we were growing up together. Like the time we put Sudocreme on Grandad's glasses when he was asleep. What age was I? Four maybe, or five, which means that James would have been six or seven. Grandad got up and walked straight into the wall and we nearly bust a gut laughing, the pair of us. Or the time we stuck a couple of dog biscuits onto the tray for Aunt Betty and she whomped them into her like they were the tastiest thing she'd had in weeks.

Only not tonight. Tonight he's taken himself off without so much as a goodbye. I sit and wait for him to appear again. I stick on a bit of Snow Patrol see if that entices him back. He's a big Snow Patrol fan.

'James,' I call. 'You there?'

A ghost taking the hump, where would you get it?

I t's not as though I consciously decided not to go out or anything. A party is organised and I intend to go. I notify my folks, tell Rhona and the other girls in my class I'll see them there, but when the time comes ... well, when the time comes I'd usually rather stay home and dance.

Tonight's the night, however; the local rugby club disco. Get the shellers off my back if nothing else. The last thing I need is to be hauled off to some brain quack, after all: *Now Jessie, how do you reeaaally feel about your brother's death?* Oh no, you can keep my share of that, so it's out and about tonight, back into the vibrant underage social scene. A good chunk of my year at school is here, along with a lot of the older ones. Dad always shakes his head in wonder when he drops me off.

'See the skirt that girl there is wearing?' he says. 'I've handkerchiefs at home that have more material in them.'

Yeah, it's some scene all right. No sign of the big spudhead yet, but he'll be along, I suppose. He wouldn't want to miss this. His old girlfriend Natalie is coping with her grief, I see. God, she cried buckets at his funeral. I was so proud of Mum and Dad that day, they were so dignified. And me? I never shed a single tear. I told myself that maybe it would have been different if James and I had gotten along, if I was going to miss him in any significant way, but as it was, I never felt the urge. And it's nice to see his old buddies having a good time; James wouldn't have it any other way, I reckon. Only it must be hard for him, watching all this; it must be hard when you're already on the way to being forgotten.

Louisa is here. Amanda and Lizzie too, telling Louisa how stunning she looks tonight in her new pink dress; Richie had another good day at the races apparently. Dad would have a heart attack if I ever set foot outside the house in anything like that. Even Alan is here, or 'The Dorkster', as Rhona calls him. Whatever else about Alan you can't fault him for good humour. All that stuff he puts up with during the school day and here he is exuberant as ever. He really is irrepressible. All decked out in his best dudsies, if he wasn't whizzing about the place so desperate to please he probably wouldn't look half bad.

'Nee-naw,' Rhona says when he's on his way over. 'Dorkster alert.'

'Hi, Alan,' I say.

'Want to dance?'

'I don't dance,' I tell him.

He grins.

'All you ever do is dance,' he says.

'Rhona will dance with you,' I tell him.

Rhona elbows me.

'He wants to dance with you.'

'That doesn't mean he won't settle for second best. How about it, Alan? Any chance you'd bring Rhona here out for a twirl?'

'How come I'm only second choice?' Rhona wants to know. 'How come you didn't ask me to dance?'

Alan's not sure what to say to this and I bail him out.

'We're wallflowers,' I tell him.

'We're too cool to dance,' Rhona says.

'Thanks for asking anyway,' I say.

We settle back to watching the scene. The hoolies are pairing off with Louisa's pals, Max with Amanda and Ed with Lizzie, best of luck to all of them. Teenage love, as Rhona always says, it's enough to make you want to puke. Still, there are worse places to be than standing here watching.

No sign of James, mind you.

I doubt he's gone for good. He'd tell me if he was going, I imagine. Not that it makes much difference either way. What surprises him most is that there was no one waiting for him. It's not as though we don't have any relatives who died or anything. Gran, for instance, there was no one in the world like James for Gran. She found it next to impossible to arrive at the house without some gift or other for him. And then at Christmas he'd get a top of the line rugby ball and I'd get some crappy doll like you'd get with a happy meal or something. Or that cousin of mine who died as a baby. I used to think about him a lot, wonder about him, hope he was okay. James says there's a whole other world out there only he can't seem to get into it. There's no one he recognises. *Hang around a while*, they tell him. He has to be ready.

No rugby, that has to be an adjustment.

Maybe it hurts to come here. Natalie with someone new, his friends exactly as they were before. Not that he's missing much tonight. It's the Richie and Louisa show out there on the dance floor, with Max and Ed and Amanda and Lizzie as the supporting cast. It really irritates me. They're performing some idiotic parody of our *Grease* routine, cracking up like it's the funniest thing ever. I don't know why it irritates me so much, but it does. It's not as though those clowns are on the dance team or anything and here they are making fun of the routines. Each of the three couples is doing the 'You're The One That I Want' routine, Lizzie and Ed really giving it socks when Amanda goes on her ear. It's pretty funny, I have to say, the way she falls over.

In fact it's more than funny, it's hilarious. When I turn to Rhona she's doubled over laughing.

'Did you see that fall?' she gasps.

Disco music stops for no one so they have to lug her outside.

'This scene is too good to miss,' Rhona says. 'Who knows? If no one's watching we might even be able to give her a kick while she's down.'

And it's all drama outside. Amanda is propped up on a bench saying, 'Ow, ow, ow, someone pushed

70

me. Who was it who pushed me?' and Lizzie is saying, 'There, there, it's going to be all right,' and Louisa is saying, 'Oh this is just lovely, you're my dance partner, why does everything always happen to me?'

Rhona, of course, is having a royal good time. If they could guarantee this sort of entertainment we'd be here every week.

And then all of a sudden the Bonzo appears, sporting that usual dopey expression of his. He raises an eyebrow.

'Take a bit of a tumble, did she?' he asks.

'Any chance I could walk you home?' Alan says.

The last song has been played and we're all standing outside.

'You off your rocker?' Rhona says.

'My dad's collecting us,' I tell him. 'You want a lift?'

'*You* off your rocker?' Rhona says to me.

71

'Got yourself an admirer?' James says.

'Shut your mouth,' I tell him.

'You talking to your brother again,' Rhona wants to know. She shakes her head in wonder. 'Just as well it's not a cab we're getting. Mightn't be able to fit us all in.'

Rhona and I hop into the back. Dad can man mark Alan in the front. They're made for each other, the pair of them, one who barely says a word, the other who never shuts up. It doesn't take long for Alan to hit his stride. In no time he's introduced himself and he's yabbering on about something or other.

I look out the window and there's James messing about, pretending he's on the rugby pitch, sidestepping in and out between the punters. Indeed one of my earliest memories of James playing rugby was the time he started showboating.

He was no older than nine and he didn't know any better, I suppose, gliding over the try line only not bothering to ground the ball, making them chase him back out again before dancing through the bodies a second time and touching down, that big smile turning to panic when he saw Dad march onto the pitch. Dad heaved him onto his shoulder and strode off towards the car. I was running along behind, simultaneously thrilled and terrified.

'The game's not over,' James cried.

'It is for you,' Dad announced and kept right on going.

Three weeks he spent on the sideline. I remember the coach pleading, Dad as polite and indifferent as you could get: 'I appreciate your situation, but I'll be the one who decides when he's allowed to play again.'

No negotiation, no persuasion.

Know what the stupidest thing was? Word got round the rugby club, the school, the neighbour-hood about that incident and everyone thought Dad was a real disciplinarian. They thought he was a hard case. But he wasn't. He was the ultimate softie. He was your average stuffed gorilla of a dad, perfect for bashing the hell out of. When I was small I'd climb over the top of the armchair and he'd say, 'Not now, Jess, I'm reading the paper,' and I'd say, 'Tough, that's your problem,' and I'd dive down on top of him and call out, 'Help, James, he's got me,' and James would call, 'I'm on it,' and I'd hear the trample of the footsteps coming from upstairs and along the hall and James would throw himself from the doorway and we'd set to work. Dad would complain that he was just home from work or that the paper was getting wrecked, but we'd have no mercy. We'd pummel the stuffing out of him. We'd drag him to the ground and we'd bounce up and down on him and he'd groan in pain and we'd bash him some more. We'd demand a submission. We'd demand an apology for being the rubbishest Dad in the world. We'd make him beg for mercy. After we'd worked him over good and proper we'd poke and jab him to see if he was still alive and then, all of a sudden, in an absolute flash, he'd sweep us into his giant arms and toss us gently onto the couch and he'd tickle us while we squealed with the purest joy. 'Apology?' he'd cry. 'We'll see who deserves an apology around here.'

Every day was the same. Five past six each evening he'd come through the door. He always seemed in such a hurry to get home, to see us again. James and I would be waiting. Not that it was always such fun in that house of ours. There were times when James and I would really go at it. We could fight over anything – the telly, the couch, where the last slice of cake had gone. That people carrier we got, we never quite found out if the folks bought it so they could help out giving lifts to rugby matches or whether it was to keep the pair of us apart.

'He poked me.'

'She poked me.'

'His feet smell.'

'She's chewing in my ear.'

'I can't see out the window with his fat head in the way.'

Not that we still have it, these days. The people carrier, I mean. Without James it was like a bus so we sold it. These days we own a Nissan Primera which is what we're in now, big family car with all the legroom Dad needs. Sometimes I sit up front next to him; more often I stay in the back and it sometimes happens when we're driving along, everything nice and peaceful apart from the easy drone of the engine and the hum of the radio and I hear this quiet choking sound up the front and I know it's coming, that same great wrenching sob and he has to pull over and the sound escalates until he can barely catch his breath. He bangs his hands off the steering wheel or maybe even his head until the storm passes and the sobbing subsides into a quiet weeping. Finally he says, 'Sorry, Jess', and I don't know what to say so I just touch his shoulder and say nothing.

Sometimes when he gets home after work his eyes are red and I think that's the worst. I picture him pulled in at the side of the road, weeping silently while the other motorists pass, on the way home to their wives and their husbands and their children, home to *Coronation Street*, to the Champions' League.

All of which seems a million miles from here. Looking at this now you'd think it was just a normal scene, a normal family. Alan's still going at it up the front. It's funny how well you can know your own dad. He hasn't said a word in minutes, hasn't been able to get a word in most likely, but I know he really likes Alan. I know from the way he's sitting, from his breathing, the way he holds the steering wheel.

Rhona grins at me.

'You reckon your dad's still alive up there?' she says.

7

Monday, 4:15. Another school day has passed and the gym is free. Free, that is, apart from Alan, or as Rhona continues to call him, 'The Dorkster'.

'Six weeks,' he says.

'That's right.'

He can't believe it. Torn ligaments, that's a minimum of six weeks. Amanda's a goner so someone else is going to have to take her place. Alan is terrified, apparently. What's he terrified about? This is my big chance, he reckons.

He could help me practise if I like. He could turn on the CD player.

'I have a remote,' I tell him. 'Anyway, a lot of the time I don't use music.'

'Water?'

'Brought my own.'

'You need someone to dance against?'

'You off your rocker?' I tell him. 'You could injure me.'

'Okay then,' he says and he shuffles off. It's funny to watch. He reminds me of one of those droopy-eyed dogs from the cartoons. Bassett hounds or bloodhounds or something. I sigh.

'You can stay if you want,' I tell him.

His face lights up. 'You want me to?'

'I don't care what you do, Alan. But there's no law against watching someone dance, I suppose.'

'I'll work the music,' he says. 'And tell me if you want a drink.'

So we start.

After ten seconds the music stops and I have to tell him, no, I'm not thirsty yet. And that's when James appears, just steps through the wall, bold as you like, same as ever, going on with his usual guff about how he used to be king of the gym, king of the bleep test, how the machine damn near exploded trying to keep up with him. He studies the scene and his usual dopey grin is replaced by – who would have thought it possible? – an even dopier one.

'Does my younger sister have an admirer by any chance?' he says. 'And more to the point, have I, as elder brother to said girl, given my approval to any such relationship?'

'Not you again,' I say.

Alan stops the tape. 'I didn't say anything,' he says.

'I was talking to my brother,' I tell him.

'Oh,' he says and I can almost see the cogs of his brain clicking into action. He goes to press the button on the CD player again, then stops.

'Did your brother not die earlier this year?'

'Does that mean I can't talk to him?' I ask.

'Yeah, does that mean she can't talk to me?' James wants to know.

'Shut that fat gob of yours!' I tell him.

'You talking to him?' Alan wants to know.

'Both of you. Now start the music again.'

I'm in no mood to brook any argument. National dance finals this day next week and I'm stuck here with these this pair. Things are not looking good. A brother who flat out won't shove off with himself and some other clown who no one seems to want around – how on earth am I going to get any practice done today?

Alan turns to the CD player and then back again.

'Can I say hello to him?'

'Sorry?'

'Can I say hello to your brother?'

'He can't answer you.'

'Can he hear me?'

I say to James: 'Can you hear him?'

'I'm a ghost. I hear everything.'

I turn back to Alan. 'He can hear you.'

Alan puts on this other world voice and calls into the distance. 'Hello there!!!'

James laughs. 'Hello there, Plonkhead.'

'Nice to meet you,' Alan calls out.

'You haven't met him,' I point out. 'You can't even see him.'

'Or hear me,' James says.

'Will you shut up?' I shout at James.

Alan wants to know if that's directed at him and I tell him it's directed at both of them and now, if he'd be so kind as to flick on that CD player since that's what he's here for, after all ...

He turns back to the CD player; he's just about to flick it back on when James, the cretin, comes out with the beauty of all beauties.

'Did I say you could have a boyfriend?'

'What?????' I shout, appalled.

'I said, "Did I–"'

'I heard what you said.'

'Then what did you say "What" for?'

'He's not my boyfriend,' I tell him through gritted teeth.

'I'm her friend,' Alan announces.

'Who said you were my friend?' I ask.

'Yeah,' James says, 'who said you were her friend?'

Then, believe it or not, James puts on this fake trailer trash American accent and says, 'Roberta May, you get back inside that there house now.' He's having a royal old time all of a sudden. 'But Ah love 'im, Billy Ray,' he says, acting out the parts, 'Ah really do love him. Get off ma leg, Roberta May, how'm Ah meant to fill that boy's backside full of buckshot with you swingin' outa my leg?'

Alan is just looking at me wondering what's going on. It must be amazing to him, watching me have a conversation with an empty space, hearing one half of it. But he seems to be able to go with it. James is grinning, pleased as punch with his little impromptu drama when all of a sudden the atmosphere changes, that change registering in Alan's expression immediately. Richie has walked in, Max and Ed in tow. I don't know what they're here for but I don't like the look of it one bit.

'What a sweet little scene,' Richie says.

'Such a cold world out there and then we go and come across something like this,' Max says.

'Heartwarming, no other word for it,' Ed adds.

Alan stands up and walks across and says,

'Hey, guys,' trying to bluff it out, but I can see his knees trembling and he's about to say something else when Richie says,

'I thought I made myself clear last time around.'

'What?'

'You suffer from memory loss? Or is it some sort of mental deficiency?'

He bounces the base of his hand off Alan's chest. 'Run!'

I tell Richie to leave him the hell alone. Alan's courage, whatever little there is of it, has seeped away again, and he stands bewildered, terrified, wishing he was anywhere but here.

Wishing he was anyone but who he is, most likely.

Richie makes out as if he's going to flick him in the eye again.

'Run!' he whispers and as Alan turns he boots him in the backside and Max and Ed laugh. I can see it Alan's expression, the pain and the fear and the self-loathing. His mouth opens slightly, but the words won't come and then he is gone.

Leaving me here alone. Apart from James, that is. Richie crosses the floor in my direction. The others follow. James's gaze follows them and then he launches himself through the air.

'Oh no, buddy boy, you don't lay a finger on her.' He flings himself at Richie and sails straight through him, Richie as unaware as could be of his presence and I can hear the anguished cry.

'No one touches her,' James cries and he launches himself again, with increased fury this time and disappears through them again.

They begin by pushing me. From one to the other and then my arms are pulled high behind my back. I don't hear if they're saying anything or laughing because all I can hear is James flailing in agony behind me.

My CDs are stamped on in front of my feet.

My CD player lands with a ferocious crash. Immediately I know that it is beyond repair.

'You just keep screwing up,' Richie says. 'That's all you have to do. Louisa doesn't want you anywhere near her. And that team doesn't need some crazy who goes around talking to herself.'

All I can do is pray that this will end soon, that the pressure on my arms will ease.

And then it does.

I hear them walk away. I don't move, I daren't until the door closes and I hear them laugh their way back down the corridor. I drag myself to my feet.

My CDs are ruined.

My CD player has been smashed to pieces.

James is sitting on the bench, the one Alan usually sits on, weeping quietly. It occurs to me how long it has been since I've seen him cry. Twenty months between us, that's all, but James always seemed huge to me. He seemed invincible.

'It's all right,' I say. 'It's okay.'

'No,' he says, 'it's not okay. It couldn't be less okay.'

'I've been bashed around before.'

As soon as I say it I know it's not true and that James won't let it pass. He stands up and strides towards the wall and then he turns and his eyes are blazing.

'Who?' he says. 'Name me one. Out on the road or in primary school, or on holidays or when you came to this place, you name me one person who ever laid a single finger on you. Who? Who, Jess, who ever caused you a moment's bother? You and Rhona and whoever you were pals with.'

'You think those jerks can hurt me?' I scream at him. 'After what we've been through since you left us? You think that?'

I see him ease back towards the wall and I see the pain cross his face like I've never seen it before and I say it:

'What the *hell* was the helmet doing on the handlebars? You moron!!! You stupid, stupid moron!!!'

But there's no point, is there? He's gone again. Maybe this will be it. Maybe he'll understand that there's nothing to be gained by his coming back again.

I turn to clear up what's left of my stuff. I hear a noise behind me. One of the cleaners maybe. Or is it the hoolies again?

It's Alan. He just stands, dumb as a rock, in the doorway and the sight of him there makes me angrier than I've ever felt before. And it all pours out of me, the most hateful bile imaginable. How he's a coward and a misfit and how no one wants him around. Or hadn't he noticed that? Why did he leave his last school? Because no one wanted him there either. His stupid jokes. That desperate neediness, did he really think we wouldn't smell it off him? Has he no idea where he's not wanted or is he just too thick to realise? All this awful stuff gushing from me and there's nothing I can do to stop it, I hurt so bad and at this moment all I want is for someone to hurt like I do and I see the pain in his face, this poor damaged kid, and I love it, I relish it and at this moment there's nothing I want more.

'YOU'RE A RETARD,' I shout at him, 'A DIM-WITTED, SOCIAL RETARD.'

I come as close as I dare. I can see his eyes fill up. His bottom lip quivers.

'STAY THE HELL AWAY FROM ME!!!' I scream into his face.

And I start to run – out of the gym, down the corridor and out of the school. I'm away down the road when the tears finally come. I run and cry. I'm bawling as I run. People just stare as I pass them.

8

Twenty months, that's all there was between us. My first memories of James? The back garden, I suppose, him and Dad out kicking or throwing a ball around. Mum and I would watch them through the patio window. And then when I finally escaped to join them, those sweet summer evenings that seemed as though they would stretch all the way into tomorrow, games of two against two, James and me against Mum and Dad, the pair of them getting a right pasting at whatever we were playing. Rugby, soccer, rounders, it didn't make much difference. Mum is really musical. Dad would always say, 'Know something, love? You catch just like a musician.'

Only it's not just individual memories that come

back to you. It's periods of time, stages in your life. Like when all I had was James and if there was no one out on the road he'd look at me and think, *Oh here, it's better than nothing*, and he'd stick me in goal. I remember our cricket set. He was always whacking the ball off the neighbouring roofs. You'd want a good technique to keep the frisbee in the garden. Golf, rugby, gaelic football, there was always something to play. And that American football outfit Gran got hold of for him. I kicked up blue murder so James let me wear the helmet and maybe it was hot underneath and maybe it didn't quite go with whatever else I was wearing but I was five or so and I liked it and damned if I was giving it back. I remember walking around the supermarket in it. I remember sitting in front of the telly in my pyjamas still wearing that helmet. James was content with the sweater, the Chicago Bears I think it was, with number 29 on the back.

Then you begin to grow up, I suppose. Grow up

and grow apart.

Time ticks by.

For years you're like twins, then all of a sudden it's as though there's a whole generation between you. Though I see him every day I still have trouble recalling his face sometimes and yet it seems like yesterday we were playing out on the road together. And it's hard to believe half a year has passed since he died.

Tuesday, 4:15.

Everyone gathers in the gym. Four more days to The National Schools' Dance Finals. You wait and wait and then all of a sudden it's upon you.

We've trained and trained all year and then before we know it we're into the last week. Posters are up. Announcements are made in assembly. We can feel the tension building. Miss Smyth gets us all together in the gym and asks what makes a team great.

'A wonderful lead dancer,' Louisa suggests.

'Not exactly,' Miss Smyth says, 'top of the list is

the ability to take knocks. And we took a real body blow last Saturday night. Amanda won't dance again this year.'

We all clap and make sympathetic noises and tell her we'll miss her and how it won't be the same without her. But to be honest we're here for one thing alone: we all want to know who'll be taking her place.

And my heart nearly stops when it's announced. It's me. Excitement mixed in with terror, that's what I feel.

'Well done, Jess,' someone says.

'Good luck, Jess,' another says.

Louisa says, 'I don't want to say anything out of place, but like, you know, is that really, like, wise? I mean, we all just love Jessie to bits and all and she does a great job on the bench, but can we really, like, take the risk?'

'I think that's probably my decision to make, Louisa,' Miss Smyth says.

'Of course it is. If Jessie was more reliable she'd

probably be on the team. I don't see why one of the backing dancers can't step in and Jessie can take a backing role.'

'They don't know the role.'

'And Jessie does?'

'She knows everyone's role. She subs for who-ever's out on any given day. And anyway, what about the tap dancing set?'

'What about it?'

'Any of the others will slow you down.'

'And Jessie won't?' Louisa says.

'No. Whatever else, she won't slow you down. She's the only one who can stay with you, even more so than Amanda.'

'Until she ends up sitting on her backside in the middle of the dance floor,' Louisa says. 'That's the whole problem, isn't it? That's not staying with someone, is it?'

Only Miss Smyth is having none of it. Her mind's made up. The tap dancing scene is going to be the clincher, the one that will swing the judges in our favour. There isn't a tapper in the country to match Louisa and it's too late in the day to change the routines.

So it has to be me.

Miss Smyth says we'll be relying on Louisa to guide me through, mind you. Maybe I should show her the bruises on my arms, ask if that's the sort of guidance she means.

'Terrific,' Louisa says. 'A whole year's work down the toilet with one stupid decision.'

In ways, I knew it had to be me. The way that scene is set up, Louisa plays a dance teacher teaching a student to tap and then when the student gets confused she heads off on this virtuoso routine of her own. It's a pretty crappy set-up in my opinion, but hey, I'm just a foot soldier. And whatever else, it does give Louisa a chance to showcase her talents. It's for the last round, the finale, where you have to have two or more on the stage and you can choose your own style of dance. Louisa and Amanda attend private dance classes together so they have been working for some time on this routine. I'll have to do the best I can, I suppose.

Amanda and Louisa and Lizzie are over the other corner of the changing room when I approach. 'Maybe we should arrange a time to practise, Louisa,' I say.

Louisa turns her back, Lizzie does the same.

'Amanda,' I say, 'you deserve better. No one has worked harder for this performance and you've had really lousy luck. I'd rather my opportunity hadn't come this way.'

I don't bother to wait for a reply, either from her or Louisa or Lizzie. I turn and leave.

Home. Exhibit B: one household racked with grief for their wonderfully gifted son.

Six months ago Mum would have said,

'Anything decent on the telly tonight, dear?'

And Dad would say: 'There's never anything good on the telly. No wonder there's so many alcoholics in this country.'

But now she doesn't even ask. Dad goes to work, comes home, reads the paper and stares at the telly. We have Sky Sports. One day about two years ago Dad came home and said, 'Fi' – that's Mum's real name by the way, Fiona – 'Fi,' he says, 'there's only one thing that can save this marriage and that's Sky Sports.' He's not usually funny like that. Mum is. That's where James got it from.

'Go ask your father,' she'd say when we'd ask could we have a biscuit. 'Tell him the answer's no and to get his backside out here and empty the dish-washer.'

Now you'll often find Dad staring at the rugby on the telly. It's as though he knows it's causing him pain, but he can't figure out where else to direct his gaze. He used to attend all James's matches. Him or

Mum, but mostly Dad. Kept nice and quiet on the sidelines too. I really liked that. Some of the parents would be going ape jumping up and down and shouting at the ref, but Dad would always stand a little way back. He never opened his mouth until they were in the car home and they would talk about the game, where James could step to cover, the angles he might run. Even after the Leinster Junior Cup final, all those other parents kissing and hugging their kids and other people's kids and each other, the first cup victory in the history of the school, and then the party in the school that night – free food, free drink, players and their families and teachers all whooping it up only there was no shifting Dad. He was the ultimate homebody; like I said already it always seemed as though he couldn't wait to get back to us. And he was always quiet, apparently. Even after international matches, which were big social occasions, you'd find him chatting quietly in the corner.

Which was how I found him the night of the final.

Only he wasn't chatting, he was just sitting alone in the front room, no TV, no music, just sitting silently in the empty room.

'You okay?' I asked him.

'You happy, Jess?'

'The whole school is happy.'

'I am,' he said. 'This is a proud day for all of us.'

Wednesday. School.

They can stick up notices about the National Dance Finals, they can make announcements at assembly and sell tickets for the event itself but school is still school. It's the same ol', same ol', only Alan is back. He was out yesterday and today he strolls in, no note, no excuse. He had a message to take care of, he says.

'Really?' says Mr Hunt, our Form Teacher. 'I'd say you might have a few detentions to take care of as well.'

Which he does. One hour after school, each day

for the next eight days. Eight hours skipped, eight hours repaid; it has a pleasing symmetry, I suppose, only I'm not sure Alan appreciates it.

I can't even look at him. I have no idea what to say other than that I am sorry, so indescribably sorry and that I don't expect him to forgive me. Words cannot be taken back and some are unforgivable. How on earth could I have said those things? I see him across the classroom. A bitter shame burns inside me.

We see out the school day. I go to get my stuff from my locker and there he is, waiting. I can't turn back. He's seen me. What is he doing here? What's the point in acting out another painful scene?

He is stupid and relentless and hurt and, I see now, extraordinarily kind.

He hands me a portable CD player. I just stand, stunned. It's not new, is it? The CDs are certainly new, still in the cellophane – *Grease*, *Fame*, 'Jazz Classics' and others, all the ones that were smashed. So that's where he was yesterday. He must have walked town looking for them.

'Alan, I can't accept–'

'Please, Jess,' he says. 'Only a few more days. You're nearly there.'

I take a breath. 'About the other evening–'

He raises his hand to stop me. 'What you said to me, you've no idea how much that hurt. But know this – it's nothing compared to what I say to myself every day of the week. You didn't tell me anything I didn't already know.' He pauses. 'I'll call by the gym once this detention is done.'

I stand and watch him walk away. All I'm left with is this shocked empty feeling. Sometimes people just stun you. Sometimes they leave you without a word to say. Chalk and cheese, true, anyone could see that but in some ways he's not unlike James. James couldn't hold any ill feeling against anyone. *Not a bad bone in his body*, that's what Mum and Dad used to say about him. No matter what happened he always seemed to give the other person the benefit of the doubt. But then again he was everyone's hero, wasn't he?

That cup final, you'd want to have seen James. He played with an unrelenting ferocity. It was as though there were three of him. Talk about being under the cosh! Wave after wave of attack, the defence stretched to the limit and any time it was pierced James would suddenly appear and crunch some poor chap in a tackle. It was as though he was an adult playing in a schoolboy game. We'd all moved behind the goal, willing the ball out. The noise and the excitement, everyone was going crazy. Hanging on, hanging on, the minutes ticking down and then he broke. I'm not sure if anyone else saw the gap, but James did, a quick exchange of passes with the win and it was like he said himself, it was sayonara he was gone, he was out of there and no going to catch him.

Yeah, whatever else about him, h was usually happy to offer a physi for this. It was to do with the pile of wet cement between his ears. Most folks, the eyes send a message to the brain which processes the information and tells the legs to hit the gears. With James, however, the danger could have come and gone and something else arrived in its place before any processing went on.

Pain too. There were times when he seemed immune to pain. A couple of years ago Dad asked me to hold a light bulb and James said, 'Mind you don't drop it there, Skinnymalinx!' and I did what any self-respecting younger sister would do, I bounced it off his fat noggin. Dad got a bit of a shock, the bulb exploding next to his ear, but James just stood there with blood beginning to appear on his forehead and said, 'Well, who ever said that girls can't throw?'

He always seemed huge. Him and Dad, there were times they seemed to dwarf Mum and me.

His shadow was long too. In school, I mean. Barely an hour in my new school and someone says, 'Hey, there she is, it's Dunner's little sis.'

'All right, Junior Dunner?'

'Hey, Dunninho, all okay today?'

The rugby lads, they were first to be on the look-out and it wasn't long before the whole school knew who I was. Those giggly girls from First and Second Year, God, what a pain they were!

'Is it not, like, you know, I mean is it not, like, just the coolest thing ever being his sister and all? I mean, you know, like, and everything?'

'No actually,' I had to explain, 'he's a searing pain in the backside most of the time and his feet stink. Much like your own brother, I expect.'

The hockey coaches were disappointed too. I could sense it. They were hoping for another super-athlete; what they got was a girl who didn't fancy a hockey ball on the knee, which would stop her dancing for a fortnight.

Second-hand glory, a mini celebrity.

Not that it didn't have its uses, I suppose. Like James said, no one ever caused me any bother. There was a group of second years who took to terrorising the younger ones, waiting for them at the back gate, and you might find the pocket of your uniform ripped or your bag emptied into a puddle or you might even find yourself face down in the mud. Good solid fun unless you were on the receiving end.

It was Rhona who first noticed it.

'Ever occur to you how many friends we have until we get beyond the back gate?' she said.

Another school day over with.

It's funny how I've become used to having him around. Alan, I'm talking about. He's in most of my classes, so I might as well just accept that I'm going to see plenty of him. Avoiding Richie and his cronies, invisible to the rest of the school and yet Alan always seems to be in good humour. In this way he is genuinely remarkable. He can't wait, he says. Soon as those doors open he's going to be there, make sure he gets the best seat in the house.

Even Rhona seems to be getting used to him. Sometimes she even forgets to call him 'The Dorkster' and uses his proper name. And the oddest thing: the gym seems kind of empty while he's serving his detentions.

Only not for long. I'm getting ready to start practice when I hear it.

'All right, Sis?'

'You back again?'

'I'm here to help,' he says. 'You remember how terrific I was when I stepped into that arena?'

It would appear that the boy has regained some of his earlier bounce. 'How could I forget? You keep reminding me.'

'How I never panicked. How cool I was under pressure. Know something? You're as good a dancer as they are.'

I laugh. 'They don't think so.'

'But you panic. That's what happens. You panic. Well, I'm here to help. Three Steps to Greatness, that's what I call this little talk.'

I ask him if he's sure it's not the Five steps to Fatness and he asks me if I want to know Step One.

'Why not start at the end of Step Five?'

'Stay in the present,' he says.

I look at him. He looks at me, pleased as punch with himself.

'Sorry?' I say.

'Stay in the present. Dancing is the same as playing rugby.'

'Really?'

'Absolutely.'

'Thirty ignorant brutes kicking the hell out of each other in the mud? *Swan Lake*? I can see the connection all right.'

James takes a breath. 'I'm telling you that the same principles apply if you want to do either one well. You have to get out of your own way. Let your body do what it's trained to do. Your problem is that you think too much.'

'And that was probably your great strength.'

'Not thinking too much?'

'Not thinking at all.'

He snaps his fingers only they don't snap and points at me. 'You're right. I never thought too much because I trusted myself. I knew I was better than everybody else. What was there to think about? But you want to know the most important principle?'

'Let me guess,' I say. 'Stay in the present.'

'Exactly. The past can't affect you. You get upset if you make a mistake?'

'Of course I get upset if I make a mistake.'

'So you're more likely to make another. Want to know a secret?'

'I'm all ears.'

'Mistakes upset everybody. Especially the most talented players since they're less likely to make them. But you know what marks the best players out from the rest – the ability to let it go. You recognise the mistake, you accept it as part of the game and you move on.'

I consider this for a moment. 'That's not really my problem,' I tell him. 'I get nervous because I expect to make a mistake.'

'So you do.'

'I do really well for so long and then as soon as I get near the end–'

'You see, that's the future,' he says. 'The past can affect you and so can the future. You think ahead. You stop concentrating on what you're doing and before you know it, you've made a mistake.'

'Which makes you more likely to make another.'

'Exactly. So you have to recognise that you're starting to think of the future and stop yourself. Control your breathing and concentrate on the moves you're performing.'

'Stay in the present. Do you know what's amazing?'

'What?'

'All the years I've known you and that's the first time you've come out with anything vaguely useful.'

'Like I said, I became much smarter after I died.' He grins at me. 'That bang on the head, it must have shaken things up in there.'

9

That day when they turned on me, the one before Rhona returned, it was probably the worst. I was stunned. It was like I'd been hit by a truck. How could I have been so stupid not to see it coming? Was it my imagination or was everyone looking at me? Where would I sit? Where would I stand? Try to keep calm, I told myself. Try not to let it show.

The trick is to make it through the school day. You make it through any way you can.

And then I made it home. James at rugby, Dad at work, there was just Mum waiting for me.

The usual words, same as any other day: 'Hey there, love. How was school?'

And the floodgates opened. I didn't intend to cry,

didn't want to. But it was the sound of her voice, I think. I began to sob. I just stood there inside the door, Mum rushing to see what had happened, and I was unable to get the words out.

Hold it in long enough, the upset and the hurt, and it all comes flooding out. I just stood there in the hallway and bawled.

I laid my head on the kitchen table and I cried. I cried and cried until it seemed as though there was nothing left inside me.

Mum listened. She didn't say much, just listened. She was very calm. She made hot chocolate and put a box of tissues in front of me. Friends came and went, she said, that was the nature of things, and maybe, if no one spoke up for me, well maybe they'd never been such good friends in the first place. The way she saw it there were three options.

I could talk to my Form Teacher about it.

She could talk to my Form Teacher about it.

Or we could see how I felt tomorrow.

That's how we worked it: we went from day to day. Tomorrow, we'd say, see how it goes tomorrow. I was lucky. Mum only worked mornings. Every afternoon I'd get home and she'd be there. Hot chocolate and biscuits and what's new in the nuthouse? Making a joke but knowing there was nothing funny about it.

The comments.

The whispers.

Parties you might have been invited to.

James never learned anything about it. God only knows how he would have reacted. Anyone laid a finger on me and he would have thumped them, no doubt about that, but with something like this? He would have been powerless. 'No Jess, no game', that's what he used to say when I first went out on the road to play. This was the first time in my life I had ever been excluded. Now it was all suggestion and gesture and innuendo. These were not things James could ever notice or understand.

And it doesn't take long for a campaign to escalate.

Leave your bag unattended and your books are covered in graffitti.

About how your father's not really your father.

Your brother's not really your brother.

And your mother, well she's the type to hook up with the first guy she meets off a plane.

And then the text messages begin to arrive.

Get off the team.

You're ruining it for everyone.

Why don't you just die, you ugly, slant-eyed bitch!

Each day Mum would be there. Some days she'd say, 'Enough, this has gone on long enough. Your father and I are going into that school in the morning,' and I'd say, 'You're right. Tomorrow it is.' Then later that evening I'd say, 'Let's leave it another day, Mum. I think I'm going to be okay tomorrow.'

And I would be.

One more day and we'd see then.

Day to day, that was the secret. Twenty minutes, she kept saying. It was the last thing I'd hear before I stepped out the door each morning. Twenty minutes from her office to the school; anything happened that I couldn't handle and she'd be there in twenty minutes. It didn't matter what else was going on. Call or text, my choice, and she'd be on her way.

It made a difference knowing she was on the other end of the phone, that she'd be waiting when I got home from school each day. Nothing upset Mum; nothing fazed her. Mum's tough. Dad, he's just a big old teddy bear, but Mum, there's a steeliness to Mum. She's so kind to people, so interested in them, but there would have been hell to pay if she had set foot inside that school.

In the end she didn't need to. It took time, but an odd thing happened. I'm not sure how but I began to cope. I stopped looking at my eyes in the mirror. I stopped feeling self-conscious when I walked. I had

Rhona, didn't I? And the school was full of kids, decent kids, ordinary kids just getting through the day like myself. The same thing kept ringing through my head. It was something Mum said. 'The Normals?' she said. 'What's normal about this?'

And it was true.

What was normal about it?

Was it normal to send those texts and to write those things or to pressurise other students into excluding you? Did Rhona do it? Did I do it? All those other kids in school, did they do it? The way Mum looked at it these kids had problems. Whatever was going on in their lives, whatever was missing, they felt the need to carry on like this. They try to make out as if the problems are with you, with the way you look, with the way you speak, the way you move. That's the most ridiculous thing. Day after day Mum kept repeating it to me. Whatever was causing this, the problem was theirs. Yes, theirs! Jealousy? Insecurity? Plain nastiness? Who knew and to be honest who the hell cared?

Yes, it took time, but I learned to deal with it. I became indifferent to them. It was something Rhona already understood or else it was just in her. She didn't give a damn what they said to her. Louisa would tell her she looked like a donkey and she'd say, *Careful I don't stand on your foot with my hoof*, and everyone would burst out laughing. Indifference, it was our greatest weapon.

Why would you send a text to someone who didn't even open it?

Why would you make a comment to someone who just ignored it?

Why exclude someone from a party if she doesn't want to go in the first place?

Dancing in front of them I still found difficult, maybe because Louisa and Amanda were the undisputed stars of the dance team. If I had Rhona with me I would have been fine. I often wished she was part of the dance team but she had no interest. So I just kept going. Day by day until it became easier. Tomorrow, we'll see how it goes tomorrow, until there comes a time when you know tomorrow's going to be just fine. It was a question of staying calm. It was a question of keeping going. It was a question of understanding that they would continue to hurt me only as long as I let them, as long as they thought they could.

Today, Louisa is in a bit of a fouler. And Rhona, I'm glad to say, is just the woman to hunt out a bit of gossip.

'Hear the news?' Rhona says, taking her spot in the canteen.

I sit into the seat next to her, peel the wrapper off my sandwich.

'What news is that?'

'The winning streak is over.'

'Richie?' I ask.

'None other. Maybe you do get better odds behind the scene, but that's no use if you keep picking the wrong horses. Know what the real question is?'

'What?'

'The ring. You reckon Louisa's going to keep it or will she send it back?'

And it's not a bad question. Louisa's not the type of girl to pay her own way or anything. Any time I've seen them out together Richie makes a big production out of paying for everything. Louisa's the type of girl who has a lot of running expenses. Make-up. Shoes. Clothes.

The way Louisa looks at it, I suspect, is that there's a Rolls Royce top of the range and there's a Fiat Punto, the main difference being that if you want to drive the Rolls Royce top of the range you have to pay for it.

A blip, maybe she reckons this is just a blip in Richie's form.

Everyone has a bad day.

The Specials, formerly the Normals, are two tables away from us here. They're too involved in their own conversation to be throwing us any dagger looks today.

'Hey Louisa,' Rhona calls over, 'that dress Richie bought you a couple of weeks back, I'll give you a tenner for it.'

Louisa's eyes narrow.

'You really think it would fit you?' she says.

'Don't worry,' Rhona laughs. 'I can always have it taken in.'

I lie on my back and stare at my bedroom ceiling. Through the past six months how long have I spent in exactly this position? We're on the countdown to Saturday. The nerves come and go. Some days I'm fine; other days I wonder how on earth I'll manage. Will I find myself lying in a heap in the middle of the floor with everyone laughing their heads off?

It's funny how the same things keep coming back into my mind. Five minutes from the end of that final, for instance, when wave after wave of attack surged towards that line, James and the rest of the team involved in the most desperate defending. You'd want to have heard the racket. The whole of First Year was behind that goal screaming encouragement. The other team's fans were roaring them on and the noise bounced around that stadium. I stood there silent, my whole body knotted with tension and all of a sudden James just turned and smiled at me. How did he know where I was standing? A scrum to the opposition, no more than five metres from the line, the tension next to unbearable, and he turns to me and smiles. How did he know where I was? It wasn't a grin. It wasn't a nervous smile. It was just the same easy relaxed smile he'd sometimes offer when the pair of us were out the back tossing a ball to each other.

That first night James came back to me I was lying awake in bed. It was in the middle of the night. He'd been gone more than a month and then all of a sudden there he was, big as you like, perched on the windowsill.

'Missing me yet?' he said. He looked across at my desk. 'I see you haven't changed your nerdy ways.'

He gave me the dopey smile.

'Go back to sleep. And don't feel guilty,' he said. 'I didn't think I was really injured either.'

Know what the worst thing is? And I mean the absolute worst here, the type of thing that tears your guts up every time you think of it. When the news came through that James had been in an accident my reaction was: *Oh typical! How inconvenient could you get?* A chunk of homework to be done, I wanted to dance and I was due over at Rhona's later. Only now the stupid clown had gone and gotten himself into a scrape with someone's front fender.

Why did things like this keep happening? Did my plans not count for anything?

No, they didn't apparently. And why? Because my brother was a dope, that's why! And what was Mum getting so panicked about? Was he not always getting himself banged about? It was part of being James and sure, he was a nuisance if he was laid up for any length of time, grumpy as hell around the house, but why all the drama?

I didn't rush to the hospital.

I didn't dawdle but I didn't rush either.

And anyway, did he not have a long history of pretending to be injured? Go out to get yourself a sandwich and when you got back he'd be rolling around the floor clutching his stomach saying, 'Intruders, intruders, I've been shot,' and I'd say, 'Give us a look, I'm a nurse,' and he'd lift his arms and I'd boot him in the ribs and he'd say, 'That's not very good nursing, you sure you're qualified?' Then he'd try to grab me by the ankles. You'd want quick feet to get past him, I tell you; if that sandwich hit the floor he'd be onto it like a shot.

What nobody really understood about my brother, what nobody really understood like I did, was that he was indestructible.

I stepped inside that hospital and it was like a whole other world. Different sounds, different smells; even the air seemed different. James had skipped A & E; they'd taken him straight to the Trauma Unit. A doctor met me on the corridor. *A serious head injury*, he told me. This was not a good situation.

Yeah, I wanted to say, *but you don't know James.*

And then it happened, this thought just came into my head. I didn't want to think it but I did: *That's my plans screwed for the evening.* It happens sometimes. This thought just shoots in before you can do anything about it.

Mum and Dad were at his bedside. Mum got up and gripped me tighter than ever before. They each had these lost, bewildered expressions. Dad reached across for my hand. James was a sight; his head was heavily bandaged and he was hooked up to different machines. My first thought was *God, it's just like it is on the telly with this little thing bleeping across a screen.*

James had his eyes closed.

How long did we sit in silence for? One minute? Two? Where were the doctors? Why weren't they running around the place?

Because he was going to be okay, that was why. No one knew James like I did. Not the doctors and nurses, not even Mum or Dad. No one knows your life like a brother or sister who is close in age to yourself. No one. No one knew James like I did.

Come on, James, you big lump! Wake up. It's not funny.

Because that's what he'd do as well. It was another routine of his – playing dead. The pair of us in the back garden and he'd pluck the ball out of the air and down he'd go and he'd lie there, nothing, not a budge. Once again, the boot in the ribs was usually the way to go with this one.

Please James, open your eyes!

Then the bleeping switched to one long continuous sound and I was waiting for the doctors to rush in.

Mum let out a cry, a piercing anguished cry.

Dad just stared, numb.

No doctors came. The next person to walk through that door was a priest.

Yes, just like that, your life changes. In a way it's destroyed. You don't just lose your brother, you lose your mum and your dad as well. They are changed forever. Grief courses through them; it's on every breath they exhale. They exist. That's all. They exist. They breathe in and they breathe out. You get through the day whatever way you can.

And in the middle of that you become a celebrity. You're the girl whose brother died. Maybe I'd always lived in James's shadow, but this was different. The concern. The pitying looks. Everyone wants a piece of you. The hugs and the tears at the funeral and that eases into a gentler concern, but life resumes its course and that's the worst bit. The funeral passes and people stop calling. All that's left is the quiet.

That awful, empty quiet.

No more texts or rumours or graffiti on my books, mind you. Some people don't know what to say so they say nothing. Others don't know what to say so they jabber on endlessly. You go from being invited to nothing to being invited to everything. Parties, sleepovers, one girl even asked me if I'd like to try canoeing. Which was really sweet. All the kindness, all the concern, all the invites, it really does mean something. But slowly life goes back to a different version of what it was. Even Louisa and Amanda and Lizzie. No texts, no graffiti, no comments about my eyes or hips. The tears turned to concern, which turned to a different type of exclusion. It was the dancing that seemed to concern them most. That was the one thing they couldn't let go.

Stay away.

You ruin it for everyone.

The National Finals, you really want to be the one to lose it?

Like I said, over a month before passed before I saw him again. It was Mum's piercing cry that woke me, like it often did and there he was, tucked nicely into that spot on the windowsill.

'All right, kiddo?'

I thought it was a one off but there he was back again the next night.

'Go back to sleep. Up and at 'em for another day's nerding tomorrow. Got to be at your best for that, don't you?'

And that wasn't the end of it. Sometimes when I'd wake he'd be there, sometimes not. There was no real pattern to it. Other than maybe if I woke frightened or upset and he'd say, 'What're you worrying for? It's all under control, little sis.'

Then one evening he pops up when I'm just settling into my homework. Night-time was one thing, this was a whole different matter. I tried to ignore him.

'Bet you miss me,' he said.

I pretended not to hear. This wasn't a road I particularly wanted to go down.

'My jokes particularly,' he said. 'I might have a few for you on the way to school tomorrow.'

The only good thing about having him back: Mum's stopped crying in my sleep. I still wake a lot. And tonight James is perched on the windowsill like he usually is.

'You got nowhere else to be?'

'Wish I did, little sis, wish I did. What do you make of the hoolies?'

'What about them?'

'They're not careful they'll find themselves in with the bad boys. Lost his winnings Richie did, and a grand to boot. Want to know why people lose big?'

I let a big yawn. Richie was vicious today; this was true. He belted Alan really hard in the chest, Alan pinning himself to the wall as they passed in the corridor, Richie in no hurry to walk by.

'They chase their money, that's why. Won't walk away, won't accept a loss. Want to talk?'

I shake my head. 'Not really.'

'Glad to hear it, kiddo. Two days, remember. Two more days and those little feet of yours are going to be tip-tapping all over that stage.'

The tap dancing scene is the one that should worry me. Only it doesn't. I know the moves, I know the beat; all that remains to be seen is whether or not I can stay with Louisa.

It's a task, I tell you. Sometimes those feet of hers are a blur.

James reckons the *Grease* scene needs a little work. 'Okay,' he says. 'Here we go. You remember Step One?'

'Stay in the present.'

'What do you mean, Stay in the present?' Alan says. He's here too, his usual spot next to the CD player.

'I'm talking to the Muttonhead,' I say.

'He's here?'

'He never goes far.' I turn to James. 'In spite of the fact that I wish he would.'

James is still wearing that rugby kit, with the black shoes. It's a hell of an outfit to be left in for all eternity. I suppose we should all be grateful he didn't keel over in the shower. There's a whole world going on out there, apparently and he's been describing it to me, folks coming and going, busy, busy. No one for him to play with, mind you.

'Ever try playing rugby with a guy who's got his head under his arm?' he says as though it's not such a big deal. 'Who knows what's going to get flipped out along the line?'

Alan wants to ask him something. When I say sure, go ahead, knock yourself out, he says, 'What's it like?' He looks way off into the distance. 'You know ... the other world?'

Which is just terrific! I'm meant to be practising and here's this clown trying to conduct a séance.

'It's lousy,' James says.

'It's lousy,' I tell Alan.

'It's like you've nowhere to belong.'

'It's like you've nowhere to belong.'

Alan thinks that sounds a bit like here. What he really wants to know is if James is the same person he was when he was here?

'He's still here in case you haven't noticed,' I tell him.

'He knows what I mean.'

'You want to now if you'll be still the same lily-livered chicken you are down here,' James asks him. Then he grins at me.

'What'd he say?' Alan wants to know.

'He says he doesn't know yet. He hasn't been dead long enough. Anyway, Step One: stay in the present. You don't think back and you don't think ahead.'

James nods. 'It's Step One of the Three Steps to Greatness.'

'Yes, the Seven Steps to Thickness. And what's

Step Two?'

'Let it go.'

'Really?'

'Absolutely.'

'That's genius.'

'You reckon?'

'You're a moron.'

'You don't understand,' he says.

'Do you?'

'Whatever happens, you let it go.' He shrugs his shoulders. 'You can't change it so let it go.'

I look at him. He seems pretty pleased with himself. 'Oh right,' I say, 'and you return to the present.'

'Exactly.'

'You're still a moron.'

'No argument there. You know when something distracts you?'

'Like Louisa bumping into me.'

'Exactly. You recognise that it happened. You say to yourself, *Louisa is a stupid cow and she has just bumped into me.*'

'And you let it go.'

'It has already happened. It can't be changed. The only thing that can be changed is how you respond to it.'

'So I should think of the future?'

'No,' he says, 'never think of the future. Always stay in the present.'

I nod.

'I have two choices. I can let it upset me ...'

'Or you can let it go. And you know how we're going to train you to do that? You're going to have to dance with Bonzo here.'

Now he's really having a laugh. I saw Alan bouncing around at the disco last Saturday night; it's a wonder Amanda was the only one who ended up at the hospital.

'You're not serious,' I say.

'I'm completely serious. I might even join in myself. If you can dance with that much distraction you can dance under any circumstances.'

And we start. I tell Alan he can dance if he wants and he says, 'Great, I'm in!' and jumps up off the bench. First up is 'You're The One That I Want' and they both think they're John Travolta, poncing about the place and flicking back their hair. Maybe James is right. If I can dance under these circumstances, I can dance anywhere.

Every now and then I wince when I think they're going to crash into each other. Only James sails straight through him, grinning. The song quickens and so do I and it's strange, for the first time in such a long time I feel at ease, dancing here with these two galoots, neither of whom has the slightest idea what he's meant to be doing.

James smiles at me.

I smile back.

If nothing else, he seems to be enjoying himself.

Dinner with the shellers.

'Nervous?'

'Not too bad, Dad.'

'Only two days now. It's normal to be nervous.'

'Were you nervous?'

'Everyone's nervous before big games,' he says. 'There's something wrong if you're not nervous,'

'A little nerves are a good thing, aren't they?' Mum says.

'As long as they don't cripple you, Jess,' says Dad.

'That's right,' I say. 'As long as they don't cripple you. I don't suppose you have any advice as to how to stop that happening, do you?'

'No. No one's ever come up with that, I'm afraid. You sure you wouldn't like some support?'

'Yes,' Mum says, 'we'd love to watch you dance.'

'Thanks, both of you. I'll be fine on my own.'

When I see James the next day he has some news. He's met someone. It takes a moment for me to understand that he's talking about his other world, his new world, and that he's met someone interesting there. It's not some floozie he's talking about either, but a relative of ours. I wonder if it's our cousin who died as a baby – I really would like to know that he's okay – but no, it's our great-grandfather. He looks a little like James apparently only not as tall. He was wearing an army uniform which doesn't bode well for James getting a change of outfit.

He told James he has to be ready. That's what he said: *You have to be ready.* They talked about sport. James comes from a long line of sportsmen if this chap is to be believed; it's only the sport that changes. James asked about his grandmother. *Hurry up*, the guy said, *if she doesn't get hold of you soon she's going to burst with the excitement.*

His other news, however, concerns this world. Richie has borrowed a chunk of Louisa's savings and has blown it, trying to win his own money back and now he's got himself further into debt. I tell him I already know. Rhona has her ear to the ground; she's monitoring developments. She noticed all the pow-wows Louisa and Amanda and Lizzie have been having, not to mention Richie and the boys going around the place like they're looking to bash some-body's head open.

As Rhona always says: Stay out of the kitchen unless you want to get burned.

As James always says: Stay away from the big boys until you're ready for them.

James says to Alan: 'What do you think?'

One night to go. I've spent the guts of an hour making sure there's no kinks in the *Fame* number and it's time to move on. The school is quiet at this time of the evening; just the three of us and the cleaners, I reckon.

'Well?' I say to Alan.

'Well what?'

'He wants to know what you think.'

'I think that was great.'

I'm not so sure. 'We're getting there,' I say.

'That's my sister, the perfectionist,' James says. 'I think it might be time for Step Three.'

'Of The Ten Steps to Uselessness?'

'Something like that,' James says. 'You have to recognise that the time for practice is over.'

Alan begins to pack his stuff; he must be due home. 'What'd he say?'

'I'll tell you later.' I turn back to James. 'Of course the time for practice is over.'

'So accept it,' he says. 'That's Step Three. You have to stop thinking about how you can improve. This is the time to perform. You just blank your mind and let your body do what you've trained it to do.'

'You can always improve,' I tell him.

'Sure you can. But not by thinking how when you're meant to be performing. I think you're ready,' he says.

'I'm as ready as I'll ever be to dance opposite Louisa. I wonder why she hates me so much. You got any idea?'

'Beats me,' James says. 'Ask Bonzo.'

I ask Alan if he has any idea. He has just finished packing his stuff. Often while I dance he does his homework only he never puts a book back into his bag before he takes another one out. So he has this tidy up at the end. I like having him here. It can be lonely dancing sometimes, always on your own, but you don't want anyone to distract you either. Out in the school in general he can jabber on a bit maybe, but here when it's just the two of us, he always seems to know when he needs to be quiet, when I'd like to talk. Now he's smiling and he says, 'Of course I do.'

'And?' I'd like to know, after all.

'And what?'

'And why does she hate me so much?'

'She doesn't hate you. She's just jealous.'

'Jealous???' I burst out laughing. 'Have you seen her? She's gorgeous. And she's a champion.'

Alan tightens the buckles on his schoolbag, hoists it onto his back.

'You asked,' he says.

'Yeah, I know. Silly me!'

'She knows how good you are.'

James pipes up with: 'He's only saying that because he's in love with you.'

'Will you shut your fat gob?' I shout.

'What'd he say?' Alan says.

I turn back to him.

'He said … it doesn't matter what he said. Listen, you're a nice guy and all but you know bog all about dancing. Let me explain something to you. There's a world of difference between a national champion and some kid who can barely get onto her school team. It doesn't matter whether it's dancing or cycling or water polo or whatever. The difference is still the same.'

So that's him in the know. Jealous indeed! He's finally ready to go; it's the same old rigmarole each evening. How can it take him so long to get his bag ready? Right then, see you tomorrow and he heads off towards the door. He's almost gone when he turns and starts up again:

'You're right, you know,' he says. 'There is a world of difference between Louisa and you. Some day when I'm older I'll stick on the telly and you know, Louisa might be there dancing away and I'll think, "Hey, I used to go to school with her." And I might even watch a while. I might watch until the end of the song or until the ads maybe. But you know something, Jessie, I'd walk a hundred miles in bare feet to watch you dance. That's the honest truth. You should see yourself when you get going. It's like … I don't know, it's electric. It's like you're on fire. There are times I'm watching you and there's this burning at the back of my throat and I get this stinging at the back of my eyes. Yeah, you want to know the difference? I watch Louisa and you're right, she's brilliant, the things she can do. I could never do them. Who wouldn't admire that? But when you dance, Jessie, it's different …… it's like magic.'

He steps through the doorway and is gone. I just stand, stunned. What a loon! Maybe he got a bang on the head as well as that dozy brother of mine. I begin to sort through the CDs, searching for the track I want.

'What a dope, eh?'

James says nothing. Maybe he's as stunned as I am. I stand and watch the door Alan has just exited through.

'You hear me?'

'I heard.'

'I said, "What a dope, eh?"'

I turn to James as he passes through the wall and disappears.

I can't get it out of my mind. James lying there in the hospital and me thinking of how my evening had been ruined. I think of him constantly. *No Jess, no game*, the words constantly ring through my head. I think of how bewildered he must feel, wandering between the two worlds, wondering what he did to deserve this. He says he's caught; he's left this world behind and yet no one wants to know him in the new one. I picture him asking other kids if they want to play and they walk straight past him. That's the worst bit. Or maybe a game is already underway only it's always full.

All James ever wanted to do was play. Shove food down his gob and play. His games were never full. And it wasn't just on the playing field that he included people. Some character stuck on the edge of a conversation and James would ask him a question. A pretty dopey question a lot of the time, sure, that goes without saying, but he always gave it a bash. And he remembered details about people – if they had a dog, what their folks did, if they had visited somewhere interesting. Which was pretty amazing since not much else stayed in that thick head of his. Ask him if there were any messages and he'd say no, not a one, and then you'd find out that five different people had phoned looking for you. Rhona says the school changed after James died. Even the older kids, they all looked up to James; whatever example he was willing to set others were likely to follow.

One thing I don't miss, mind you, is those pals of his and the way they'd descend on our house. God, the noise! Enjoying a nice *quiet* joke, are we, boys? No, not a chance. It would be *Har! Har! Har!* And then they'd be punching each other on the shoulder. Or else high-fiving like they'd just come up with the funniest thing in history. And what about the slamming doors? See how it works, pal? Press the handle down, close gently, then release the handle. No need to rip it off the hinges now, is there? And you'd want to have seen the buggers eat. They were like a swarm of locusts. Come in after they'd gone and there'd be nothing, not a morsel, everything scoffed. The best you might get would be some crumbs where one of them would have got so excited, he'd have forgotten to take the wrapper off a packet of cream crackers before attacking it.

Now it's quiet. There was a time when my house was one of constant noise interspersed with occasional pockets of quiet; now there seems to be an endless silence which hangs over each room. No matter what noise there is, the silence dominates.

Still, I suppose, there are no distractions for a girl waiting for the biggest night of her life.

Stay in the present.

Let it go.

Just perform. The time for training is over.

If you listen closely enough all you can hear around here is the clocks tick.

11

The National Schools' Dance Championship; the culmination of a whole year's work as Miss Smyth keeps telling us. Control the controllables; that's what James used to say. If you can control it, control it; otherwise let it go. What's the point in worrying? The only time he ever got nervous, he said, was when he was unprepared. If you'd prepared yourself for a game, after all, why wouldn't you be looking forward to it?

And funnily enough, that's how I feel. Nervous, sure, but if I fall, I fall. If I make a fool of myself, I'll have to accept that. The sun will still come up the following morning, won't it? But somehow that debilitating terror of performing in public has left me. There's no going back now so I might as well just go for it.

Not that everyone has the same confidence in me. We get our stretches done and we move in for some last words from Miss Smyth and it's then that Louisa whispers it to me:

'I can see you making a show of yourself tonight. I can see you going down real easy.'

I'm momentarily stunned. Even now, even at this late stage, but I can't change it and I can't change Louisa so I just shrug and let it go. Something is not right though; the atmosphere on the team is different. Jessica Kinch who is a gabber of the first order, who is normally a little tornado of energy before a practice, let alone a performance of this importance, is stone silent. Is she sick? She doesn't look sick. She looks dead and dispirited, as though someone has just let the air out of her. I make eye contact as if to say: *You okay?* She just looks at me vacantly for a moment and then turns away.

And Adam Lyons, he's different as well though

I'm not sure quite how.

Are there others? The other boys on the team, for instance, is everything as it usually is with them?

More to the point, however, where is James? The big dope would be here by now, I imagined; where else is he likely to be? Who else would want him around? Only no sign.

What is wrong with the others?

It's a huge auditorium and the first rows are reserved for the performers to watch. First up are Whitechapel High. The way it works: there are three rounds, each school performs three scenes and the draw means that we're last in the sequence. Which suits Miss Smyth, she says. At least we'll know what we have to do.

If James were here he'd understand that there was never any doubt about what we had to do. The sequence of events changes nothing. The way to approach things is to put everything else out of our minds and dance as well as we can.

Whitechapel are well drilled and their routine is good, but their nerves show. Everything almost comes off for them; their timing isn't quite right. And the lead, to be honest, is nowhere in the same class as Louisa. Other performances come and go. They're all very good, competent and well prepared, but nothing really stands out ahead of the others. With Blackhall Academy who are second favourites after ourselves, the lead is excellent and the performance is good, but the whole arrangement is the type we've all seen a thousand times before.

If we all perform, and if Louisa does her stuff then we're in with a real chance here. We are the favourites, after all.

And it goes well. The *Fame* routine is first. We are nothing if not well drilled. It starts with Louisa moving between us singing, like she's a young hopeful making her way, which is what the story is about, I suppose. And then we all peel away, split into pairs and provide a backdrop for her to do her stuff. Even I have to admit that it's nicely choreographed. I'm holding my own too, in and out with Louisa, focused on the now, nothing but the now and then all of a sudden it happens: Jessica Kinch goes down. I'm stunned. Jessica is a really steady dancer. It's just as well it's me she goes down in front of because I'm quick enough to adjust and not bring the others down with me. She climbs back up and finds her way back in, but the damage is done, any advantage we might have had has gone; one fall, Jessica of all people, and it is as though we are all level again. Or maybe even a bit behind.

Back in the dressing room Jessica can barely look at us. She is terrified to meet Miss Smyth's glare. Miss Smyth is trying to be upbeat, to get us to put it behind us, but her anger shows. At least she has the good sense not to attack Jessica.

And then James pops up. *Good of you to make it? Bit of a bottleneck with the rest of the ghosties, was it?* Only James doesn't look much like James tonight as he sits over towards the edge of the stage. I've seen him angry and sad and furious and elated; I've even seen him frightened when we were younger. But I've never seen him dispirited. I've never seen him look beaten before.

All we can do is sit and watch the others go through their second routines. This time Whitechapel are stronger; they have calmed. It's a decent routine, a 1930's jazz piece and it's well performed but sometimes you need someone like Louisa to bring it to a higher level, don't you?

Blackhall are no better than functional; the lead doesn't stand out so much this time and there's every chance that they used up their best routine early to make a good initial impression on the judges.

Which leaves the way open for us. We are ready; we are pumped. People are urging each other on.

'Let's have it, gang,' Miss Smyth says.

'It's there for us,' another says. 'No mistakes this round.'

This time it's the *Grease* scene, Louisa blasting her way through 'You're The One That I Want' with Daniel Block all slicked up like John Travolta, Daniel well able to sing and a good enough dancer that he doesn't impede Louisa. The rest of us are in the secondary roles, Louisa's friends or Daniel's pals and it's a good routine again and Daniel's playing a stormer offering just the right foil for Louisa until he collides with Adam Lyons, and it happens so suddenly that it stuns me. They haven't collided all year. Adam is a really solid dancer, completely reliable. And it's then that I'm sure, it's then that I know exactly what's going on.

I'm sticking on the taps when he appears.

'It's a fix,' I say. I don't even look at him.

'That's right, little sis. Crooked as a two euro note.'

'Richie?'

'The one and only. Swimming with the sharks and looking to pay some of what he owes back. Your lead dancer too. She's looking to recoup some losses. Know why they didn't pick you?'

'Why?'

'Louisa reckons they don't need to. She reckons she can tie you in knots.'

I shrug. 'Maybe she can.'

'And make you fall.'

I try to smile at him. 'Stay in the present, eh?'

'No,' James says. 'This is the time to forget about the present. Think of the future. Richie's a bad one and he's getting worse and I'm not around to look after you. You know what you're going to do?'

'What?'

'You're going to go down when they want you to. You've got your whole future in front of you, remember.'

I don't know what to say to that so I say nothing. It's extraordinary that this is what it has come down to. Richie is in deep. Either he has bet heavily against us winning or he has guaranteed a bookie that he can fix it so we don't. Either way he has to make sure we lose.

'Make the smart move, Jess,' James says. 'This is one to walk away from.'

Numb, I sit and watch. Routines come and go and I barely notice. The rules for this round are simple: any dance you want with two or more dancers. Whitechapel go for a different *Grease* routine to ours and it's not bad and Blackhall send a girl and a guy out onto the stage to do some jazz number. They're not all that talented, but they're brave and they give it everything they've got and the audience love them. Then it comes to the last dance of the evening – Louisa and me. I can feel the butterflies in my stomach. I concentrate on my breathing, slow it right down, like James taught me to.

We stand side by side, ready to step out onto the stage. We are wearing top hats and each of us holds a cane.

'Careful you don't hurt yourself when you hit the

ground,' Louisa says and we step out into the lights.

For the first part of the piece, Louisa is showing me how to tap. She starts with a simple ball tap and a heel tap and then runs them off one after the other and I follow. I can sense that the audience like the idea; and they'll get the chance to watch Louisa perform without the rest of us in the way. She performs a couple of ball digs and heel drops first with the left and then with the right and then combines them to make a cramp roll and then she does the same again only precedes it with a brush and I follow suit.

We move back and across the stage – tap, tap, tap. Louisa hams it up a bit with her hands on her hips when she's watching me and the audience acts like it's actually funny. Louisa then combines two brushes, one forward and one backward, to turn it into a shuffle and then she does it again but shortens the movements to make the step faster. I do likewise.

I feel good. It's as though my mind is completely blank. All that is working at the moment are my eyes and feet. Louisa's eyes are fixed on me but it's as though I see right past her. Off we go again.

We are both equally focused, I suppose, me on the dance, Louisa on getting her money back. And maintaining her reputation. She and Richie have it all worked out. The bookie makes a killing and forgives the debt; Louisa emerges with her reputation intact. She has performed heroically; it is other less talented and less committed dancers who have let her down.

She tries a couple of Broadway-style shuffles and then the quicker hoofer-shuffle with its double tap sound and the audience applaud and I do the same and they applaud some more. She tries to make eye contact with me; I just follow her feet. There is a sweet irony here: the more she tries to shake me off, the better she has to dance; the better she dances the more chance we have of winning.

She abandons the set routines.

It is around now that I am meant to throw my arms up in admiration and let her at it.

Back and across we go again. I can see it in her face, how much she wants to shake me off, how much she wants me to fall. Tap dancing is pretty much a set number of steps – all that varies is the sequence and the way they build upon each other and as I watch, as I follow her, I realise how well I know her sequences, that she only has so many variations, that she has been taught them well, that she has learned them well, but they are all that she possesses.

Sometimes that's enough if you can perform them quickly enough.

And sometimes it's not.

Over and back we go.

She increases the pace and yet it's as though she's dancing in slow motion. What previously seemed a blur to me is nothing more than a set routine.

And then I do it. She has routines and signals that let me know the next step, so why wait for her?

Now we are dancing together, dancing in time and the crowd is loving it, the noise is terrific with all the cheering, but the funniest thing is that it's so quiet inside my head, the noise seems distant and I'm not thinking about anything, I'm just letting my eyes pick up Louisa's signals and letting my feet follow my eyes.

I can see James in the distance. He's not cheering, just as I wasn't cheering when he made that break in the cup final. His face is drawn with tension, just as mine was; his stomach is in a knot just as mine was. Where the supporter experiences excitement, the brother or sister experiences agony. That's why he smiled at me. He was saying, *It's okay, Sis. It's all good*.

I smile at him.

It's okay, you big spud. It's all good.

And back and forth Louisa and I go again.

It's now I see the panic register on her face. The money. The surprise and the embarrassment of seeing me match her had caused her to momentarily forget. If she can't make me inadvertently throw the competition, she will have to do it herself.

Can she afford to let her money go and feed Richie to whoever has been lending to him?

Can she afford to damage her reputation by falling?

But she has the props of course.

It's the cane that goes first. It has hardly bounced before I have it flicked up with my own cane and placed back in her hand. She stares at me in astonishment.

Her top hat has barely skidded to a halt when I tap across to it, tap on its edge to flip it up and catch it with my own cane. Louise stands with venom in her eyes. I tap my way back again and, using the cane, place the hat squarely back on her head again.

Somewhere in the distance, somewhere in the quiet I can hear the crowd respond.

I can see Louisa's panic increase. She can't shake me off, she can't make me fall and now even the props are no help. There is only one thing left for her to do: she will have to take a tumble herself.

Back and across we go.

And again.

I wait.

And then we fall, both of us, as close to being synchronised as makes no difference, that slightly lazy left side of hers being the giveaway, the left foot brush ball change the obvious one to go down on. I watch for it, read it and down we both go together.

The crowd goes completely silent.

Louisa begins to rub her ankle.

Everybody just watches. Is this part of the routine?

Louisa has no more than five yards to limp. I remain motionless until she has gone. I'm here alone on the stage.

Almost total silence.

I wait. I'm not ashamed to say it: I'm milking the moment.

Then I flip myself up and tap, tap away again.

How do I finish the performance? There is

nothing rehearsed, it's just me on the stage under the fire of the lights only it doesn't feel like that, it feels like I'm at home in my room happily dancing away before the shellers became the shellers, back when James's booming presence still dominated my home.

It reminds me of when he made that break in the final, wave after wave of attack and then he saw the gap, made the ground, tossed the ball out then got it back at just the perfect moment and then he was gone, I tell you, he was gone, out of there and no one was going to catch him, no one even tried and the crowd was going crazy, I don't think I've ever heard noise like that in my life and I wanted to scream too only what I wanted to scream was: *That's my brother, you know. That's my brother.*

Maybe it's because he's a ghost or maybe it's because he's James, but he doesn't have any inhibitions.

'That's my sister,' he cries out to the crowd who can't hear him.

And I dance on. My feet know what to do; they will know when to stop. I feel the energy of the crowd pass to me and then back to them and back to me and back to them.

Tap, tap, tap, I feel as though I am flying.

I am mobbed by my teammates when I come off. They are whooping and cheering and Miss Smyth bashes her way through and tells me I'm a little gem, that she recognised my talent and plucked me from obscurity and where would I be without her and this is the start of wonderful things for me. Louisa's sore ankle is of little interest to anyone. What most people want to know is: Have the judges made a decision?

And they have.

We've won.

Not by much. We were further behind than I thought before the last round. But we've won and all of a sudden everyone's jumping on each other again.

Back in the changing room, mind you, things are

more subdued. Louisa flings her things into her bag and marches out. To her parents maybe. Or to Richie? She doesn't even bother to limp.

All of a sudden I want to be at home. A party is due to take place tonight, arranged by one of the parents, but right now I want to be at home. With my folks for a while, sure, but also up in my room, just me and James talking about what happened tonight.

The dressing room is still charged with tension. It is clear to me that Louisa tried to throw the competition, but does everyone else know? What about the others? Were they threatened and if so, how many? Are they worried about the consequences? Maybe Adam and Jessica are scared that they didn't do enough and that there will be recriminations. Louisa has grabbed her bag and left. Lizzie has followed her.

At the door I stop and say, 'If anyone asks you what happened just tell them I twigged it and threatened to go to the police.'

I could get a lift, but at this moment I'd like to be

alone. It's only one bus journey home, and not such a long one at that and there's a bus stop just outside. I leave through the back entrance, the one nearest to the bus stop and that's when I hear a voice I recognise:,

'If it isn't Little Miss Loner! Even in her moment of triumph, no one wants to be with her.'

It's Louisa, of course.

Only Louisa isn't the problem. There is six of them: Louisa and her two chums, Amanda and Lizzie and the lads as well, Richie and Max and Ed, all standing in a group, unsmiling. They are intent on trouble, it seems. Is it me they're waiting for?

Can I outrun them? Is there the energy left in my legs.?

I don't get a chance to find out.

The voice behind takes me by surprise. It's Alan and his voice is choc full of excitement as he says, 'Hey, Jess, you're not sneaking away on–'

And he sees them.

He looks from me to them and then back again. Panic has registered on his face; he understands that he would rather be anywhere but here.

Richie tells him to beat it.

I can see the fear take control of him. He wants to try to bluff it, say *Hi guys* or something like that, only he can't get the words out.

Richie says, 'You deaf? Get the hell out of here.'

Still Alan stands. Is he so terrified that he cannot move?

'I said, GET THE HELL OUT OF HERE!!!'

Alan stands.

And Richie hits him a slap. It's a hard, open-handed slap, a humiliating slap for one boy to receive from another. Alan doesn't raise his hands to protect himself.

It's not that he can't move.

He won't.

Another slap. Harder this time. The sound rings out like a shot. Still Alan stands. I can see his knees and hands tremble. He won't run, he won't speak, and he won't defend himself.

'RUN!!' Richie screams.

Only Alan won't budge. Richie says; 'You really want this?'

Still no reply from Alan.

Can't run? Won't run? I have no idea which.

Richie raises hand again only this time Alan catches him by the wrist. For a moment they are stopped in time, their eyes locked. Then I hear Richie's name being called and I turn and it's Rhona standing there only she's not alone, there's the whole dance team there and some others too, other kids from the school who have come along to support.

We stand and stare at each other.

Nobody moves for a moment. It's as though they can't quite believe what they are seeing.

Seconds pass – I have no idea how many.

And then something extraordinary happens. It's Amanda, of all people, who makes the first move; she goes tap, tap across on her crutches, out from behind Louisa to join her schoolmates behind me and Alan. Louisa stares in astonishment, then in horror.

Amanda stops and says, 'I'd have given anything to be up there tonight. Absolutely *anything*. All the nights I lay in bed and it was all I could think about. Same as everyone else on the team. Know something, Louisa? If that wasn't enough for you, I don't want anything to do with you.' Amanda turns to Ed. 'You can make your choice.'

Ed makes the choice. He follows his girlfriend across.

And Lizzie follows him. She says, 'Know something, Louisa? You're an awful bloody cow. Everyone worked really hard for this competition.'

Louisa just stares, stunned. Max shrugs and says, 'You're on your own, man,' to Richie.

He turns and walks away.

Richie and Louisa just stand isolated.

'That's just beautiful,' Louisa screams at her two

friends. 'You're jealous, that's what it's always been, you've always been jealous of me.'

Her voice has a pitiful, plaintive quality to it.

'Go home, Richie,' Alan says. 'You've no business here.'

And they all troop back inside. The show, as they say, is over. I watch them go one by one until it's just me and Alan and Rhona and Rhona says, 'See you out front, Dorkster,' and then it's just me and Alan.

I'm not sure what to say to him. His eyes shine. He seems at ease, in a way I've never seen him before.

'You going to the party?' I ask.

He nods.

'You going home?'

'I want to see my mum and dad. You're not going to be rushing off, are you?'

'You going to come along?'

'Dad might drop me up later.'

He gives me a big, broad smile.

'I might be there,' he says. 'In fact I might be sitting by the door waiting.'

12

Sometimes the sweetest part is the morning after when you wake and remember the night before; the excitement has passed and you are left with the deepest satisfaction which warms you inside, intensely at first, then less intensely, until your mind makes room for it, accommodates it, and you begin to look forward again, towards the next dance, the next challenge. For now, though, I'm happy to sit here at my desk and enjoy the sensation.

A science test on Monday. First day after we've won The National Schools' Dance championship and I'm here studying for a Science test.

And waiting for James. He'll be along, I'm sure of it.

There'll be a big presentation at assembly tomorrow. Miss Smyth telephoned; she wants me to lead the team onto the stage but I declined. I thought Jessica would be a good choice. Either her or Amanda. The whole team will be there; maybe even Louisa if she's not at the doctors having her ankle seen to.

Rumours were flying about Richie today. Rhona really has a talent for ferreting out this sort of information. Nobody is quite sure how much he owes, but apparently his old man is going to clear the debt. Luckily his family are not short of a few bob. But the big news is that he won't be coming back to our school. Word has it that he's going to be heading to boarding school down the country. Which of course begs the question: Are there no decent boarding schools in Australia?

And Louisa, what about Louisa? She will have woken to a different world today, one that will take a bit of getting used to. But she will get used to it, I suppose. Maybe people will learn about how she tried to throw the dance competition and maybe they won't. Whatever the case they won't learn it from me. Louisa has enough problems at the moment without my adding to them.

My phone's been hopping. Texts have been flying in, kids in my year mostly, offering their congratulations.

Where is James? I wonder.

And no sooner have I thought it than there he is. He pops himself onto the windowsill, his usual spot. Is he missing a little of that usual spark? I ask him what's wrong.

No reply.

'Cat got your tongue, eh big guy?'

It's as though he can't find the words. And then he does, only haltingly.

'Want to know something?' he says. 'They were right. All those folks who'd come up to Mum and Dad and tell them it must be so exciting for them, having a champion in the family like that. Only it wasn't me, Jess.'

I look at him.

'You're crazy.'

'It's true.'

'What about The Three Steps to Greatness?'

'I could never put them into practice, not like you. I only looked like a champion, Jess. That happens sometimes. Appearances can be deceptive. I would have been found out. I was bigger and faster and stronger than everyone else, but sooner or later the others would have caught up. You should have seen yourself go, little sis. All that pressure on you and for you to be able to perform like that. Your name's going to be up in lights. There'll be folks queuing down the street to see you dance.'

At this moment I know that I have never felt closer to him.

'With you next to me I feel I can do anything,' I tell him.

And then he says it.

He looks at me and says, 'Oh, I won't be next to you.'

Just like that. Words I can't bear to hear. Words

that still twist my gut even though I was half expecting them.

'No. Don't say that.'

'That's the way it has to be.'

'I don't want to hear it.'

He turns his palm upwards and smiles.

'I'm dead, remember.' He looks around a moment, then he says, 'I met Gran.'

'She's been waiting for you?'

'She wants to know if you remember Tigger?'

'Of course I remember Tigger. Gran was minding us. Mum and Dad were at a wedding.'

'I got a ball.'

'Yet another ball. And I got Tigger. That big vase bit the dust that night.'

'It was your lousy catch.'

'Your lousy throw, more like.'

I'm not sure what I feel here. Dread? Relief?

'So she's been waiting for you.'

'They all have. Some guys asked me if I wanted to

play rugby yesterday.'

On another day I'd ask him if anyone had his head under his arm. Or wouldn't the guy with all the chains around him struggle? Now, however, I find it hard to get the words out.

'Can I ask you something?' he says.

I don't answer.

'You know that big hole that's been there in your heart since I died – that any smaller now?'

I tell him I don't really know. A little maybe.

'It'll heal, you know,' he reassures me. 'Each year it'll get a little smaller until it'll just be a tiny little dot and you'll be able to live with it. You have to start letting the folks come to watch you dance.'

I have already broached this matter with Dad. He and Mum are welcome to attend next time I dance in public. 'It'll never replace watching you play rugby,' I tell James.

'It doesn't have to. Dad'll be like you. That awful pain will ease and all that'll be left will be the sadness.

He'll learn to accept things.'

'And Mum?'

He shakes his head sadly. 'She'll keep doing what she's doing. She'll breathe in and she'll breathe out. I'll be in every thought she has, every movement she makes. That pain will always be with her. But she still has you, Jess.'

He grins at me.

'Hey,' he says, 'you remember that poem you made up about me?'

'There's no one quite as useless as a brother?'

'That's the one.'

'One's enough, who needs another.'

He grins.

'You sure you haven't changed it around a bit?'

'But find yourself in tears / And he'll put away your fears.'

'Hey, that's more like it.'

'Only the problem with mine is he's a total spudder.'

He smiles again. I think he prefers that one. I tell

him I don't want him to go and he says that he can't even begin to describe how much, and I cut him off and tell him that doesn't mean I want him to go all sappy on me either. He laughs and I laugh and then I rush across the room and bury my face into his chest.

'I can almost feel you again,' I tell him. And it's true. I can almost feel him.

'I know.'

'I don't want you to go.'

'I have to, little sis,' he says. 'I have to.'

Then he eases from my grip and fades through the wall.

'Goodbye,' I whisper. 'Goodbye, James.'

Once he has gone I settle back to my desk. Yes indeed, a science test tomorrow. Evaporation is the process by which molecules in a liquid state become gaseous, if you don't mind. What about that then?

I ramble downstairs to see the shellers, get myself a sandwich. Yes, James is gone. But somehow I feel as though he will never be far from me.

And the doorbell rings.

I wait a moment to see if anyone budges.

'Does no one ever answer this door except me?'

I know who's calling mind you, and there he is with this big grin and he's nerded up his hair for a laugh, just like Rhona and I did that first time we met him.

He steps inside and musses it up again, back to its usual messy state. Ever so gently I touch the back of his hand with my little finger.

'Mum? Dad? There's someone I'd like you to meet.'

TURN THE PAGE

FOR MORE GREAT BOOKS FROM

THE O'BRIEN PRESS

Dear Diary,

I'm in despair! I'm in exile, stuck here in the remote countryside ...
If it wasn't for Jenny – who is the shiniest, happiest girl in the world
– life here would be unbearable.

Oh well, between the two of us I'm sure we'll manage to have some
fun this summer!

**Welcome to Tia's summer, which ends up being *much* more
exciting than she imagined!**

My name's Tammy and I'm 15 years old.

I've decided that this summer I am going to spend more time at the stables – sometimes I think the horses are the only ones who get what I'm all about. If only moody Martin wasn't always there, but I suppose I can put up with him. Just.

Dear Diary,

I have NO friends.

I mean you'd think that I could make one person like me after six months here ...

Ever since her family moved to the country to live on a farm, Poppy's been miserable. She has a new life and a new school, but unfortunately no new friends. Luckily, that's all about to change...

JUDY MAY

'I'M STILL WAITING FOR
MY CLOSE-UP!'

D S G
GIRL
DIAMOND
STAR

My name's Lemony, I'm nearly 15, and this is my journal. Things I like: my best friend Ro, Nick Collins, reading and hanging out with friends. Things I DON'T like: my glasses, the way I talk too fast around boys …

Anyway, Ro, my brother Paul and I are going to have fun working on the film set in town – as long as boring Stephen Brown doesn't try to hang out with us …

Welcome to Lemony's summer: Lights, camera, action!